A. A

D0334340

993103886 1

fearless

fearless

TIM LOTT

WALKER
BOOKS

This is a work of fiction. Names, characters, places and incidents are either the product of the author's imagination or, if real, used fictitiously.

First published 2007 by Walker Books Ltd
87 Vauxhall Walk, London SE11 5HJ

2 4 6 8 10 9 7 5 3 1

Text © 2007 Tim Lott
Cover images (pb) Robert Daly/Stone/Getty Images (girl)
and Jeanene Scott/Photonica/Getty Images (rose)
(hb) *Christ in the Sepulchre, guarded by Angels* by Blake, William (1757–1827)
© Victoria and Albert Museum, London, UK/The Bridgeman Art Library
Illustrations © 2007 Clifford Harper/Agraphia.co.uk

The right of Tim Lott to be identified as author of this work has been asserted
by him in accordance with the Copyright, Designs and Patents Act 1988

This book has been typeset in Fairfield

Printed and bound in Great Britain by Creative Print and Design
(Wales), Ebbw Vale

British Library Cataloguing in Publication Data:
a catalogue record for this book
is available from the British Library

ISBN 978-1-4063-0862-4 (pb)
ISBN 978-1-4063-0858-7 (hb)

www.walkerbooks.co.uk

To my four beautiful children,
Ruby, Cecilia, Lydia and Esme

"Always be brave. Always be yourself."

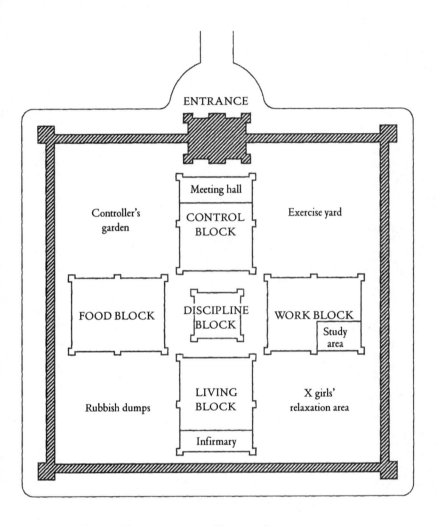

ENTRANCE

Controller's
garden

Exercise yard

Meeting hall

CONTROL
BLOCK

FOOD BLOCK

DISCIPLINE
BLOCK

WORK BLOCK

Study
area

Rubbish dumps

LIVING
BLOCK

Infirmary

X girls'
relaxation area

CITY COMMUNITY FAITH SCHOOL FOR
RETRAINING, OPPORTUNITY AND HOPE

Prologue

The Night They Came

The girl could hear sobbing in the front room. Her mother was always crying about something or other, so the girl didn't take much notice. She just kept staring at the vidscreen in the corner of her bedroom. There was an advert for a holiday showing, all blue sea and white waves and sand like a field of honey. She wished she could just climb into the vidscreen and stretch out on the sand, dip her toes into the water and never return. She would stay there and watch the world from the other side of the screen.

Then the knocking on the front door began. The girl thought that was odd, because they had a perfectly good doorbell. The knock seemed almost like a message. It went *rap-rap-rappety-rap*, as if it was a friend or a neighbour who always did their own special knock. But friends never came after dark, and the neighbours kept themselves to themselves.

The girl heard a noise behind her. She turned and saw her mother. A dark birthmark the size of a fingernail and the

11

shape of a star protruded from her hairline. Her cheeks were still damp from crying; her eyes were red and scrunched up like meat from a butcher's shop. She hadn't answered the door. Instead she lifted the girl up and pressed their faces together. The girl kissed her mother, and tasted salt. Her mother smiled, as if to tell her that everything was OK. Then she said she had some presents for her. The girl didn't understand. Her birthday was months away.

Her mother produced a small cloth bag, and brought out three objects. The first was a picture of the girl's grandmother and grandfather, mounted in a bronze frame. Her grandfather wore a black suit with a cravat, and her grandmother wore a long pale dress and a floppy dark hat.

The second was a beautiful old silver watch with a fine leather strap that she said had once belonged to the girl's father. She said she ought to have something to remind her that she did once have a father.

Finally she gave the girl one more thing. A golden locket containing a tiny photograph of her mother on her wedding day. She hung it gravely around the girl's neck. Then she put the framed photo and the watch back into the little cloth bag, handed it to the girl and kissed her.

The knock on the door came again, louder this time. *Rap-rap-rappety-rap*.

Her mother left the room. The girl heard the door catch being released, and then her mother began to shout. She heard a man's voice, stern and official sounding.

A few seconds later, a man in uniform wearing a black peaked cap walked into the girl's room and, without a word, lifted her up. She could hear her mother crying. The man didn't pause to let her say goodbye to her mother. He started to carry her down the stairs. The girl went limp. She felt unable to speak.

The door closed behind her. Then she heard her mother's voice through the thin panel of wood.

"The locket. Read the words. Never forget the words on the locket."

In the harsh light of the street, the girl studied the back of the locket. She could just make out three lines of faint engraving. The girl pushed the locket inside her blouse, and closed her eyes. She didn't resist as the man bundled her into the back of the ugly grey car with no side windows, started the engine and drove away into the darkness.

The Institute

*When everyone has freedom,
no one has freedom.*

The Controller

"You're in trouble again, Little Fearless," said Beauty, idly inspecting her perfect fingernails, their cuticles like pink crescent moons, as the girls walked slowly out of the Control Block. The Sunday Gathering had just come to an end. She began smoothing the tips of her nails with a tattered scrap of sandpaper.

Now that the Gathering was out of the way, the girls had a few hours' free time before they were given a meal in the Food Block. Some of them were returning to their halls in the Living Block in order to catch up on sleep; others flopped down where they stood onto the hard ground of the exercise yard.

Soapdish, her scrubbed dark skin like polished mahogany, nodded gravely in agreement with Beauty. "Have you noticed how the Controller picks on you, Little Fearless?" Protruding from the breast pocket of her drab cotton drill overalls was a small, threadbare, black rag doll, with grey button eyes and hair made out of strands of wool. Soapdish had brought this doll with her when she had first come to the Institute and she treasured it above everything else.

"Why should he pick on me?" said Little Fearless. She fiddled distractedly with the battered old purple beret on her head. Then she absent-mindedly picked her nose, one of her less savoury habits. She was also untidy and washed less often than some – particularly Soapdish – thought she should. She almost looked ugly – until her hypnotic, mysterious eyes opened wide. They were extraordinary: one was turquoise blue like a southern sea, the other so brown the inky-black pupil was swallowed up by the iris.

"Because he knows trouble when he sees it," said a voice from behind them.

It was Tattle. She was tall, lithe and athletic, with shoulder-length fair hair compressed into tight natural curls. Her ears stuck out slightly and sported generous, fleshy lobes like purses of flesh. She turned to Little Fearless.

"LF, you must be crazy mad. Why d'you want to get yourself into hot water like that? You know the Controller's got it in for you, but you go and stir it up. I can't believe you sometimes. You must have ice water for blood. I wonder what they'll do to you? The old man looked bent right out of shape. On the other hand, you never can tell with him, can you? Maybe Lady Luck's coin will land in your favour. I didn't like the look of her, though, writing away in her little notepad. Oh, I hate her more than any other X girl. I hate her more than Bellyache or the Whistler or even Stench." As usual,

Tattle didn't stop talking until she was out of breath.

The four Y girls, Beauty, Little Fearless, Soapdish and Tattle, stood around in a ragged circle. There were only girls here; antisocial boys and young male juvies were expelled to the Outlands, far from the City. It was hard to tell the girls' ages, but none were yet women, and all were old enough to walk and talk and, most importantly, work – like the rest of the thousand girls in the Institute. The girls worked six days a week, dawn till dusk, in the giant laundry which occupied most of the Institute building known as the Work Block.

A fifth figure, a Z girl, appeared behind Little Fearless, having broken away from the mass of the other Z girls, the youngest and most recent arrivals, who made up the bulk of the Institute's population. They got the worst jobs, and the fewest privileges. The Y girls were often snobbish about mixing with the lower-letter girls, but occasionally Z girls were befriended by the older ones. This girl had become close to Little Fearless, and so was tolerated by Beauty, Tattle and Soapdish.

Like the rest, she didn't have a real name – not the one she was born with – just a letter and a number, which were roughly cut into bracelets locked around their wrists at all times. All the girls were forced to leave their real names at the gates of the Institute and were forbidden from ever using them. The Y girls had steel bracelets, but this girl's bracelet – since she was a Z girl – was brass. It was inscribed Z242, but she was known as Stargazer, because she liked nothing better than to gaze at the stars which could be seen wheeling and glittering through the pane of a small solitary skylight in the roof of Hall Seven, where she slept with Tattle, Beauty, Soapdish, Little Fearless and ninety-five other Y and Z girls. The X girls, of whom there were only fifty, had their own separate quarters in the Control Block.

When Stargazer spoke, it was so quietly that Little Fearless had to strain to hear her. The younger girl had pale, almost transparent skin and watery, greenish eyes. Little Fearless sometimes joked that she could almost see through her – as if she were actually made of the starlight she loved to peer at through the high window. Her hair was the colour of corn, and was by far the most beautiful thing about her.

"Will they put you in the Discipline Block, Little Fearless?" Stargazer murmured, her pale hands shaking slightly. Her high forehead, which when she was asleep was as smooth as a lake on a windless day, now rippled with lines of worry. Little Fearless didn't respond, but gave the younger girl a quick squeeze of reassurance.

"What made you do it?" asked Beauty, grimacing and showing the gold tooth that glistened under the awning of her perfect scarlet lips. "It draws attention to us all, you know – not just you."

"That's not fair," said Stargazer softly. "I think standing up to the Controller like she did was brave."

When the Controller had asked at the end of the Gathering if there were any questions, Little Fearless had had the nerve to ask one – two, in fact. She had asked the Controller why they had to work so hard when they were only children, and why they were locked up when most of them had done nothing wrong. The Controller had been furious, and had left without answering.

Soapdish immediately rounded on Stargazer, a tiny fleck of white spittle appearing on her dark, almost earth-coloured lips.

"What do you know, *Yellow*? You don't know the difference between being brave and being a fool. You just worship Little Fearless because she protects you. Why don't you just slink back to your Z friends and have a game of hide-and-go-seek or ring around a rosy or something?"

There were girls who called Stargazer Yellow. For some it was because of her bright yellow hair, but mostly it was short for Yellow Belly, or coward. She was scared of everything – scared of her dreams, which were vivid like prophecies; scared of the other girls; and scared of the future.

"Please don't call me Yellow," begged Stargazer.

"Quite right," said Tattle cheerfully, and she sprang forward to within an inch of Stargazer's face, letting out a loud "Boo!" Stargazer jumped and yelped in surprise.

Tattle giggled, her face radiating mischief. "You're scared of your own shadow – *Yellow*." She tried to catch Beauty's eye so they could be partners in teasing Stargazer. All the girls tried to curry favour with Beauty because she was the best-looking and most popular girl in the Institute.

Stargazer hated herself for it, but she felt she was about to cry. She looked away, hoping no one would notice. Now it was Beauty's turn to chip in. She turned her head towards Tattle, causing a ripple in her perfect straight hair, black and blue like midnight. Her skin was the colour of milk chocolate. Her small, slightly upturned nose was pierced with a single silver stud.

"Stop bickering. What's done is done. Little Fearless is our friend and we need to stand by her. And Stargazer is Little Fearless's friend, and so we should try to be kind to her. But I still would like to know, LF – why *do* you always seem to want to bring trouble on yourself?"

They all looked at her – down at her, in fact, because she was several inches shorter than any of them. She was tiny for her age, and scrawny.

Little Fearless looked steadily back at Beauty and wiped at a speck of dirt on her face with a grubby sleeve, extending the speck into a smudge. Then she said, "I hardly know myself. Partly, I think, it's something to do with the Controller. It's as if he wants me to stick my neck out, so he can chop off my head. It's almost as if he's daring me. And I find it hard to resist the challenge. I can't explain it. There's something that—"

Little Fearless stopped talking as her arm was suddenly gripped in a vice-like hold. She winced, and turned to see the X girl they called Bellyache standing behind her, face like a sour lemon. The other four girls shrank away. As they had expected, talking back to the Controller at the Gathering meant that Little Fearless was headed for the Discipline Block once more.

"Get lost," muttered Bellyache.

Little Fearless gave a barely discernible nod to her friends, and they melted away into a knot of other children who had gathered to see Little Fearless being marched off. Bellyache made an angry face at the crowd and they quickly dispersed.

Bellyache, her narrow horsy face grimacing, had not let go of Little Fearless's arm. As always, she slouched, carrying her wide shoulders low as if buckling under the weight of gravity.

"What did I do?" said Little Fearless angrily. "I haven't broken any of the rules."

"You'd best shut up," replied Bellyache. "You've got yourself into enough trouble as it is with your big mouth, Little Useless."

Pinching her arm, Bellyache pushed and shoved Little Fearless towards the squat, threatening ugliness of the Discipline Block. It was painted black and had a flat concrete roof. It was the size of an ordinary house, but had no upstairs – only a ground floor and a cellar.

"I did a few shifts there this week," said Bellyache, poking Little Fearless in the ribs to move her along faster. "Every time, it seems to get worse – colder, darker, damper. Bad enough in there as a guard. It's like a punishment being sent to babysit you dribbling brats. I shouldn't like to be locked up in one of those cells, I've got to say, though. The rat problem's getting worse – they come over from the rubbish dumps and burrow in – and the toilets are all blocked up, so it stinks something terrible too. I hate it there. But then," added Bellyache almost cheerfully, "I hate it everywhere."

Little Fearless hugged herself as a sharp wind swooped over the low walls and bit into her flesh. She was not afraid of the Discipline Block – she knew the Controller wouldn't leave any girl in there long enough to do her any long-term physical damage in case it made her less efficient as a worker – but she let out a sigh of resignation as she contemplated yet more days in a draughty, lonely cell.

"Walk faster, Little Hopeless. You never walk fast enough. You're lazy and slack, like all the Y and Z girls."

Little Fearless flashed her a defiant glance and refused to change her pace, which was already so brisk she felt she was about to break into a run.

"Don't you dare look at me like that," snapped Bellyache. "Think you're so tough, don't you? Well, the Controller's got plans for you. Not that way, Little Clueless. This way."

Little Fearless had automatically wheeled towards the entrance to the Discipline Block, a route she had taken many times before during her long stay at the Institute. But on this occasion, Bellyache spun her round and pushed her towards the rear entrance to the Control Block.

Little Fearless was surprised – and a little anxious. In all her years here, she had never been inside this part of the Control Block, where the Controller and the X girls lived.

It was strictly forbidden for Y and Z girls to come here. Her mind began racing. Was there another place of punishment, perhaps, even uglier and colder than the Discipline Block?

The door to the Control Block was immense, and made of solid iron. It creaked loudly when Bellyache pulled it open. Inside, there was a dimly lit hallway, semicircular in shape, with four corridors leading off it. The second had a sign above it that read CORRIDOR ONE. The third was corridor two, and furthest to the right was corridor three. All these led to where the X girls lived and worked.

The first corridor, on the left, was numbered zero. Little Fearless assumed, correctly, that this led to the Controller's office. He didn't have a letter, but he had a number, and that number was zero.

"We'll be going along corridor nothing," muttered Bellyache irritably. Clearly she didn't like the idea of going there. There was a dead smell to the air, and the lights that illuminated the cramped corridor flickered yellow and orange, giving the impression of perpetual twilight.

After several minutes of marching in silence, the corridor opened out into a huge hall, an anteroom at least thirty feet high, with a domed ceiling. Bellyache was sweating profusely, either from exertion or from nervousness. In front of them were tall double doors made out of thick, old wood and carved with numbers between one and a thousand. At the centre of them all, encircling the door handles, was a large carved zero.

Despite her sweating, Bellyache was also shivering. "I'm cold," she grumbled. "Give me your jacket."

"No," said Little Fearless matter-of-factly.

Bellyache, who was a good foot taller than Little Fearless, and the same amount wider, grabbed a handful of the copper-red hair that straggled out from under her beret.

"Give it to me!" With her other hand, she reached for her scourge. The scourge was a heavy leather strap that all the X girls carried, which they used to discipline anyone who got out of line. A single stroke of it would leave heavy welts, and sometimes break the flesh.

Little Fearless wriggled away from her furiously. "I won't. It's mine. You're fat enough to keep yourself warm."

Bellyache went red in the face and clutched at Little Fearless with her grubby fingers stained yellow with nicotine; Bellyache, like most of the X girls, smoked. But at that moment, although neither of them had knocked on the door, there came a voice from within the Controller's office.

"Enter."

Bellyache immediately stopped what she was doing – which was twisting one of Little Fearless's ears between her finger and thumb – and hissed, "Behave yourself." With that, she smoothed down her smart uniform: deep navy jacket, jodhpur-type trousers, knee-high chestnut leather boots and small military-style cap with a crescent peak. Then she slowly opened the door to the Controller's office.

Little Fearless, determined to show some spirit, marched in quickly in front of Bellyache, as if positively eager to meet the Controller, who, outside of the Sunday Gathering, rarely spoke to any of the Y or Z girls directly, leaving it entirely to his lieutenants, the X girls, to communicate his orders.

The room was square and very large, perhaps thirty feet from wall to wall, but there was barely any furniture in it. The Controller sat behind an immense desk attending to a pile of paperwork. He looked thin and washed out, as if he'd been put through the laundry a dozen times and had lost all colour and shape. There was a single wooden chair in front of the desk, smaller and lower than the large, carved one in which the Controller sat. The room itself was clean and tidy, but not in any way pleasant. There were no pictures or decorations other than a large City flag on the wall behind the Controller. This featured a clock, to symbolize the brevity of life and the urgency of struggle; a muscled arm, to symbolize the importance of work; and a single eye, to indicate the all-knowing god of the City, Eidolon. Superimposed on the pupil of the eye was the symbol of the Ten Corporations, a bundle of ten sticks tied together with a piece of string. It was meant, the girls had been taught, to symbolize strength through unity.

Bellyache gestured sharply for Little Fearless to stand next to the low chair, which she did, upright and proud, looking directly at the Controller. Without glancing up, the Controller snapped at Bellyache to leave. And leave she did, sloping and slouching out of there as fast as her hefty legs could carry her, almost slamming the door behind her in her haste.

The Controller was wearing his usual dung-coloured suit and plain grey tie. The few strands of his dishcloth-coloured hair that remained were plastered across his scalp; there was a snowfall of dandruff on his shoulders. Little Fearless felt she could almost smell him – a cross between washing powder and gravy. He wore, as he always did, tinted spectacles that hid his eyes.

He finally looked up from his papers and beckoned for her to sit down. Little Fearless remained bolt upright.

"I'd rather stand if it's all the same to you," she said, her voice loud, clear and unfaltering. She didn't like the fact that sitting down in the chair would make the Controller tower over her, and make her feel even smaller and more helpless than she actually was.

"That's entirely your choice," said the Controller, his voice cracked and parchment dry. He returned to his paperwork.

From shadows in the corners of the room, two X girls appeared and came to stand either side of the Controller. The one to the Controller's left was tossing a coin up in the air repeatedly, catching it in her palm, flicking it over onto the back of her hand and scrutinizing it carefully. This was X1, the head of the X girls, whom all the Y and Z girls called Lady Luck. She had crawled and betrayed and bullied her way to the top, and she was the most powerful and unpleasant of all the Controller's goons, though you would never have guessed it by looking at her. She had a snub nose as innocent as a baby's, strawberry-blonde hair, a Cupid's bow, and apple-pink cheeks. Only her eyes gave her away – they were cold and seemed to reflect no light.

"Would you like a glass of water, perhaps?" asked the Controller.

Little Fearless caught the look of surprise on Lady Luck's face, and so she decided, just to annoy her, to accept the Controller's offer.

"X1, go and get the girl a drink of water."

Resentfully Lady Luck disappeared, leaving the larger, more sinister X girl in the room. She was X17: the Whistler. Tall and pale with cropped jet-black hair, she always had a faint smile on her face, as if laughing at some private, imbecilic joke. It was well known that she was a mindcrip, and one of the most dangerous in the Institute. Her skin was raw and chapped as if she perpetually stood in a freezing wind. Her eyes were not cold, like Lady Luck's, but blurry and far away. No one had ever heard her speak, only whistle nursery rhymes under her breath.

In the dead air, hissing through X17's teeth, was the end of a tune. Little Fearless filled in the words silently.

Here comes a candle to light you to bed,
Here comes a chopper to chop off your head.
Chip, chop, chip, chop…

Lady Luck returned a few moments later with a glass of water. Little Fearless examined the surface, where there was a little gobbet of foam. She felt sure that the X girl had spat in it, and put it down on the Controller's desk.

"Don't do that," said the Controller. "If you've changed your mind, give it back to X1 and she'll get rid of it for you."

Little Fearless picked up the glass and held it out. With her face showing even more fury, but still silently, Lady Luck retrieved the glass, put it on a windowsill and then took her place once more beside the Controller. She dug a cigarette out of her pocket and lit it. She blew the smoke towards Little Fearless. Little Fearless was vaguely aware of some game being played, but she wasn't sure of the rules. She remained stock-still and silent as she waited for the situation to unfold.

The Controller kicked back his chair and loosened his tie slightly. "Do you know why you are here?" he said, examining the fingernails on his right hand, which were bitten and rough at the ends.

"Of course I do," answered Little Fearless immediately. "My mother was wrongly accused of being a fomenter, a terrorist. I never knew my father. So when my mother was taken away, I was sent here to be brainwashed." Little Fearless only had a vague memory of what had happened the night she was taken away, so she had embellished the memory and now believed her own story.

To her amazement, instead of appearing angry, the Controller laughed – a thin, high-pitched sound, almost like a woman's laugh – and clapped his hands. Then his face suddenly became stern.

"Do you remember your mother?" he asked.

"I remember her," said Little Fearless bitterly. "I remember how brave she was, and how strong. And how much she loved me."

She realized to her shame that tears were streaming down her cheeks and there was a smirk of satisfaction on Lady Luck's face. Immediately she wiped them away and, almost as an act of defiance, sat down, crossing her legs insolently.

"Make yourself comfortable. Then we can get down to discussing why you're in this office. And then—"

Little Fearless interrupted him. "Why *am* I here? Why *am* I being punished? You asked if anyone had any questions, and I asked some questions, that's all."

The Controller's face darkened. Lady Luck and the Whistler glanced at one another and leaned forward like attack dogs straining at the leash. When the Controller spoke again his voice was softer but somehow more threatening than before.

"Do *not* interrupt me. One of the reasons you are in this institution is because you do not possess respect. Freedom requires responsibility, and that is what you are here to learn. You are here to learn about rules. Rules are there for a purpose. Do you believe that, my girl?"

"I don't know," said Little Fearless neutrally, trying not

to be dishonest, but also trying hard not to provoke the Controller any further.

"Well, they *are*," he snapped, leaning forward in his chair earnestly. "They hold everything together. Without rules there would be no order. There would only be freedom. And when everyone has freedom, no one has freedom."

"But some rules are so unfair," said Little Fearless quietly.

The Controller gave a dry, bitter laugh. "Of course they're unfair. That can't be helped. The point is, the worst thing in the world is not unfairness. Do you know what is?"

"Cruelty?" said Little Fearless innocently.

"No," replied the Controller evenly. "It is chaos. And since the war started, we have been constantly under the threat of chaos. Rules may be fair, or they may be unfair. Frequently they *are* unfair. But it doesn't matter. They keep disorder at bay. So we have to believe in them. Or, if we don't believe in them, at least *pretend* to believe in them, for the benefit of the common good."

He moved his tinted glasses back and forth on the bridge of his nose, fidgeting with the hinges. Little Fearless squinted through the gloom to try to catch a glimpse of his eyes, but it was impossible.

"Where is my mother?" she asked defiantly.

The Controller sighed and began doodling idly on a piece of paper. "We'll come to your mother in a moment. Let's talk about your behaviour first, shall we, Z73?"

"Y73, actually," said Little Fearless.

Now Lady Luck spoke for the first time. Her voice was musical but hollow, like a penny whistle played through a tinny radio.

"That was before you disappointed the Controller. You are now a Z girl." And with that, Lady Luck moved round to the front of the desk, reached down and roughly ripped off the cloth Y that had been sewn onto her jacket. She then unlocked Little Fearless's steel identity bracelet and replaced it with a brass one with Z73 carved into it.

"I've done nothing wrong," Little Fearless said in a voice that barely concealed her frustration. "You asked if there were any questions and I—"

"You are not being punished for asking questions," said the Controller. "You are being punished for telling lies."

Now Little Fearless felt angry. She prided herself on her honesty. "What lies?"

"Or perhaps," said the Controller, "it would be better to call them stories. Because that is how you dress your lies up, isn't it?"

Little Fearless was well known as being the best storyteller at the Institute. With no toys and few books, and little time for exercise or games, storytelling was one of the last entertainments the girls were allowed. Crowds would gather around Little Fearless whenever she told a story. So vivid and mesmerizing was her delivery, even the X girls would stop to listen.

The Controller gave a hollow chuckle. "Of course, I don't care if you make up harmless tales. But the ones you've been telling could upset and disturb many of the sensitive and troubled children we have in this institution. Especially your tallest tale about how your families are looking for you, and are all going to come and get you one day."

Little Fearless stared at the Controller defiantly. The stories she told made all the girls who heard them feel better, and stronger, and more optimistic. The one about how their families were going to rescue them one day was the most popular story of all.

"But that's not a story," she responded. "That's as true as anything."

"I'm afraid," said the Controller, "that really doesn't mean very much nowadays."

"I don't care what you say," insisted Little Fearless. "My mother *will* come and find me, as soon as she is free."

"Yes, well. That brings us to the main reason for your coming here today." He looked up at Lady Luck and then the Whistler. "Could you excuse us for a moment, please. I have something I need to discuss with Z73 in private."

Sullenly Lady Luck and the Whistler marched out into the anteroom. The Controller looked back at Little Fearless.

Something in his face gave Little Fearless a feeling that she had never had before. She felt empty and clammy. Behind this feeling was a little black thought, like a distressed bird fluttering under the surface of her mind, just out of reach.

For one of the few times in her life, Little Fearless felt afraid.

"You're a clever little number," said the Controller. "Clever enough to be a Y again one day, or even an X. Perhaps the highest X of all."

"I don't want to be an X girl," said Little Fearless quietly. "They're bullies and thugs."

"Oh, they're not so bad. They only do what is necessary. If they didn't do it, someone else would have to. Besides…" The Controller paused as if weighing something in his mind. "Besides, they at least have some sort of future," he said finally.

"What do you mean?" said Little Fearless sharply.

"I leave it to you to draw your own conclusions," replied the Controller, gazing at her intensely. "I am not at liberty to tell you everything about the Institute or how it operates. But take it from me. Working as an X girl can have its compensations in the long term. You would be foolish to deny yourself that opportunity. And if you think the X girls are thugs and bullies, then you would have a chance to make them better."

"Are you going to promote me?" said Little Fearless sarcastically. "You've only just made me a Z girl."

The Controller continued to look at her levelly. "Your future is up to you. But if you want to become someone, if you want to be a Cityzen again, you have to behave yourself. Plenty of the girls seem to manage it well enough."

He regarded Little Fearless through the lenses of his tinted glasses. When he spoke again it was almost pleadingly. "Why can't you follow the rules? Just for a few years.

You won't be in here for ever. And you could go far."

"I'm quite happy as I am, thank you very much," retorted Little Fearless. "Can I go now?"

"Not quite yet," said the Controller. "Answer me this, please. Will you give me your word that you will stop telling all these foolish stories about your families?"

"If the people in the City knew the real truth about this place," said Little Fearless, "you know they would tear down the walls. That will happen, sooner or later. My mother…"

She paused. Something made her hesitate. Before she could carry on, the Controller spoke.

"Your mother is not going to come and get you, Z73."

"She is," argued Little Fearless defiantly. "As soon as they release her."

A strange expression passed across the Controller's face. It made him look unfathomably sad. Little Fearless felt uncomfortable, because she realized that she actually felt sorry for him – and that made it harder to hate him.

After a few seconds, he spoke again. The words seemed to travel in slow motion across the air between them.

"Your mother is not going to come and get you." The Controller, who had risen from his chair and begun pacing the room, rested his dry, papery hand on Little Fearless's shoulder. "Because your mother is dead."

Little Fearless felt the weight of the Controller's hand lift from her shoulder. His words echoed in her head. They seemed meaningless, like the distant cry of a wild animal.

Then she felt a strange sensation. It was not grief – or even surprise. It was as if some part of her that had been ghostly and insubstantial had suddenly become firm and solid.

Because at that moment, Little Fearless realized that she had always known her mother was dead. She did not know how she knew, but she did. And she had grieved for her mother already, and for years. Now these words of the Controller's, instead of crushing her, seemed to free her.

"I know," said Little Fearless in a quiet, unshakeable voice. "I have always known."

"Have you no heart? Do you not care?" wondered the Controller, clearly astonished at her remarkable self-possession.

"I care," she said evenly. "And thank you. Thank you for taking my head out of my clouds of confusion. For now I realize it was the confusion that was hurting me more than anything. But if you think by using cruel facts as hammers you will break my spirit, you are wasting your time. For my mother's – my dead mother's – sake, I will survive and I will be strong. And you will never – *never* – turn me into your creature, Controller, for all your heartlessness."

Little Fearless suddenly saw a terrifying anger in the Controller's face, so intense that she feared he would attack her. Then he gathered himself, sighed, and returned to his chair. Pressing a button on his desk, he summoned the two X girls back into the room.

As soon as Lady Luck and the Whistler entered, the Controller's face went completely blank once more. As if a switch had been thrown, he returned to his normal self: dried out, emotionless, with no guts or juice. He went back to scribbling on bits of paper. Little Fearless assumed that this meant the meeting was over. She now awaited her punishment for daring to defy the Controller once again, even after he had used his cruellest weapon.

"Should we punish her, X1?" asked the Controller, without looking up from his desk. Lady Luck and the Whistler had taken up their previous positions beside his chair. Lazily, as if nothing mattered, Lady Luck tossed her coin. The other girls called her Lady Luck because she used that silver coin to decide nearly everything. Whom to punish, what kind of punishment to give them, what she was going to eat, even whether to take revenge on someone who had offended her.

"Heads, she can join the rats in the Discipline Block for a week," said the X girl with eyes cold as stones.

The coin rose in the air in a perfect arc then fell on the back of her hand. She showed it to the Controller without a word. The Controller inspected the coin, paused, then waved his hand towards the door.

"You may go, Z73."

Her luck had held out. She was not to be punished further.

"Lucky lucky. But everyone's luck runs out sooner or later, Z73," warned Lady Luck.

Little Fearless turned and walked out of the room into the antechamber, where Bellyache, sour-faced and impatient to leave, was waiting for her.

The Vision of Stargazer

Death to the City Boss!
Death to the Democrenes!
Death to the Ten Corporations!

Oroborous, from *The Seven*
*Sayings of Oroborous**

---

* *The Seven Sayings of Oroborous* is currently on the list of books designated *Samizdat* (forbidden) by the City and the Ten Corporations. Possession of this book by unauthorized Cityzens is punishable by up to ten years' imprisonment.

Later that day, Stargazer returned to her bunk in Hall Seven of the Living Block to find Little Fearless staring at a photograph in a golden locket that hung around her neck. She had not expected to find her there.

"Little Fearless. You're here! I'm so happy. I thought they would throw you in the Discipline Block." She hugged her friend.

Little Fearless stroked Stargazer's hair silently but continued looking at the locket. Stargazer noticed that Little Fearless's eyes were as sad as the last day of summer.

"What happened?" she asked, separating herself from Little Fearless and seeing what she was holding.

"He told me that my mother was dead," said Little Fearless simply. Her dirty face was marked with the track of a single tear.

Stargazer gasped. "No. Surely it can't be true."

"It is true," said Little Fearless. "I have always known it to be true in some part of me – ever since I can remember."

"What do you mean – ever since you can remember?" said Stargazer, clutching Little Fearless's hand. "You can remember your mother, can't you?"

"I can remember the woman who brought me up. The woman I was with that night when they came for me. But although I loved her, she was not my mother. I know that for sure now."

Stargazer looked completely lost. Little Fearless continued to gaze at the locket.

"The woman who brought me up had a birthmark, you see. It was about the size of a fingernail and the shape of a star, on her face, just below her hairline. She used to tell me that a star had fallen from heaven and left a mark on her. I remember it so clearly. And it's not there in the photo. Although this looks a bit like the woman I called Mother, when she was much younger, it isn't her. The woman in the photo is my real mother – I am sure of it."

"How do you know?" asked Stargazer.

"I just do," she said simply.

Little Fearless held out the photo to Stargazer. It showed the head of a woman in her early twenties. She was beautiful, with thick dark hair, enormous eyes brimming with intelligence and life, and a wide, smiling mouth. Although there was no obvious resemblance to Little Fearless, there was something about her – perhaps the brightness of her eyes, or the proud, challenging way she gazed into the camera lens – that reminded Stargazer irresistibly of Little Fearless.

"She's lovely," said Stargazer. "Perhaps she had the photograph altered so that you couldn't see the birthmark."

"The woman who brought me up wouldn't have done that. She was who she was and nobody else," said Little Fearless. "And she wasn't my mother, although she loved me like a mother."

"Your heart must be broken," said Stargazer, softly.

"No," replied Little Fearless firmly, wiping away a tear. "I cannot grieve long for someone I never knew. And I believe the woman I called Mother, who I did love, and who I am sure loved me, is still alive."

"It's so sad," said Stargazer. "But we will help you with your loss, Little Fearless. Me, Tattle, Beauty and Soapdish. We will each try to be some part of a mother for you."

Later that day, as the evening settled in, Little Fearless met her four friends in their secret place. The rubbish dumps occupied a large rectangle, maybe fifty yards long, between the Food Block and the Living Block. Running beside the dumps was a small, little-used alley where the rubbish containers were stored. It usually stank here, so most of the children, X, Y and Z alike, kept away. But the rubbish lorry had come the day before, so it didn't reek too badly. There was only one X girl usually patrolling this part of the Institute, X12, known to everyone as Stench. Stench looked after the dumps, but this evening she was nowhere to be seen.

The girls arranged themselves in a circle on the rough ground, and checked to see if they had been noticed. But to all intents and purposes they were alone.

After her meeting with the Controller, Little Fearless had decided to try to answer the question that her friends were always asking her. Why was she always getting herself into trouble with him? She told them she couldn't answer the question without telling them a story. And so they sat and listened as she told them about the night the man with the black cap had come to take her to the Institute.

They sat in silence, completely absorbed. She told them about the locket, the portrait of her grandparents and the watch that she had brought with her that night. In the car on the way to the Institute she had seen flashes of light from explosions in the distance.

"It all happened at the time when the bombings were at their worst, and the war in the Outlands was going very badly. There were even those who said…"

Here Little Fearless paused for dramatic effect.

"*Oroborous* was going to topple the City Boss and take everything over."

She whispered the name "Oroborous", even though they were sure no one else could hear. It was taboo to speak it.

"Who is Oro-Oro-Oroborous?" asked Stargazer timidly. Beauty, Soapdish and Tattle glared at her as if she were an imbecile.

"The bogeyman," said Tattle, contorting her face so she

looked monstrous. "He comes at night to eat Z girls." She turned away and picked up a black pen, and began drawing something on her arm.

Beauty looked disdainfully at Stargazer. "Oroborous is the mastermind behind all the terrorist attacks," she said, as if everyone should know this.

"No one has ever seen him," added Soapdish in a low voice.

"They say he has a tattoo of Oroborous the snake, the ancient symbol of the pagans. Oroborous was always shown curled in a circle, eating its own tail."

"Where ... where was the tattoo?" asked Stargazer nervously.

"On his *wrist*," said Tattle suddenly, thrusting her own wrist at Stargazer. With the black pen, she had drawn a serpent snaking around it. Stargazer flinched.

"Is that why they took you away from her, LF?" wondered Soapdish. "Was she a..."

Soapdish left the sentence unfinished, but Little Fearless knew exactly what she meant. Many of the girls in the Institute were juvies, young criminals who had fallen foul of the curfews and antisocial orders that rained down constantly from the City Boss. Most of the X girls, who seemed to enjoy violence, came from the ranks of the juvies. So did Tattle, who had been a petty vandal and shoplifter. But others had been seized from homes where their parents were said to be terrorists, or followers of Oroborous.

"I never believed she was a terrorist," said Little Fearless. "The authorities made a mistake, that's all. They make mistakes all the time, my ... the woman I thought was my mother said. Arresting people who haven't done anything wrong, just because their identicards are out of date, or they're heard saying something they shouldn't about the City Boss.

"But it's true she did tell me secret stories of Oroborous, who, she said, was not a terrorist at all, as the City Boss painted him, but a brave and brilliant freedom fighter, and the true friend of the people of the City. I remember she always made Oroborous seem romantic. I think I even wanted to be like him.

"I don't care that she wasn't my real mother. She was always good to me. She loved flowers, and she always made sure I had some in my room, by the side of my bed, so I could look at them before I fell asleep. She said it would help ensure that all my dreams would be good. We both loved white roses. Ever since I came to the Institute I've dreamed of seeing one again."

Little Fearless took the locket that she believed contained a photo of her real mother out from under her shirt, and stroked it gently.

"Can I read them, LF?" said Tattle, pointing at the locket. "The words on the back, I mean."

Without taking the locket off, Little Fearless turned it over so that Tattle could see the back. All the other girls craned their necks too.

"It's too faint. I can't read it," complained Beauty.

"It says: *To a true Hero. Always be brave. Always be your-self*," said Little Fearless. "I think it is a message from my real mother. And that is why I am always in trouble with the Controller. Because I have to be brave. And I have to be myself. To stay true to my mother, sometimes I have to break the rules. The Controller despises anyone who won't follow his rules to the letter, so he tries to crush me."

"Why doesn't it say your name?" said Soapdish bluntly.

"What *is* your real name, Little Fearless?" asked Tattle innocently, as if she was doing no more than asking the time. Not only was it forbidden to use real names in the Institute, it was taboo to tell another girl your real name. It was thought to be bad luck, and if the Controller found out, you could get into very hot water. They were meant to have forgotten their real names.

"I promised I would never use my real name again until I became a real person and went back to the City," said Little Fearless sharply. "All I have now is a slave name, and until I can be free, I will not tarnish my real name. Do you understand, Tattle?"

Tattle shrugged, clearly disappointed that she hadn't been issued with a prime piece of gossip. There was a long, slightly embarrassed silence, broken eventually by Soapdish.

"Are you going to do as the Controller asks, and stop telling stories about when our families are going to come for us?" she asked.

"No," said Little Fearless simply. "Because they're not stories. They're true."

"I don't see how they can be true. The City Boss would never allow it to happen," said Tattle sulkily. "Let's face it, we're stuck here, at least until we're grown up."

"There is something greater than the power of the City Boss," said Little Fearless, "and that is the love of families for one another. And I'm sure the truth about this prison – which they pretend is a school – is kept a secret from all in the City."

The Institute presented itself artfully to the outside world. A cheerful, brightly coloured sign at the front of the Institute read CITY COMMUNITY FAITH SCHOOL FOR RETRAINING, OPPORTUNITY AND HOPE.

The high perimeter walls were made of mellow pale pink stone covered with ivy. From the outside, comforting turrets and towers could be glimpsed. From the inside, the view was entirely different: the walls were black, ugly metal that reflected no sunlight and had yards and yards of cruel, coiled barbed wire stretched across their tops.

"This is why, you see, no one has come to rescue us. The City Boss has told them lies. Perhaps they have been told that we are dead, or far away in the Outlands. Or more likely they have been told that we are safe here and being helped to become proper Cityzens. So they may have given up on us, or decided that this is a good place. But a secret as big as this cannot be hidden for ever. When our families and the rest of the Cityzens find out that we are kept in a prison and treated like animals, they will tear the walls down."

"But what about the girls that return from the Institute to the City as women?" said Beauty, outraged. "Everyone must know what it is like in here, because the girls would tell everybody."

"Oh, Beauty," said Little Fearless wearily. "You know the truth about the girls who leave the Institute. You all know – don't you?"

Now Tattle stuffed her fingers in her ears. "Not listening, not listening, not listening," she muttered to herself over and over again.

"I know what you're going to say, and that's stupid," said Beauty, angrily.

Little Fearless sighed. She believed that the fact none of the girls had ever come back to visit the Institute – or told everyone in the City what was going on here – meant only one thing; and the fact that none of their families, or any of the Cityzens, had ever come to save them proved it beyond doubt.

The truth was that when the girls became women, they didn't return to the City at all, as they were promised. Instead, Little Fearless believed that they were just moved into other institutes, institutes which were for women instead of girls and which were probably just as bad as the place they were in now.

"It doesn't matter," said Little Fearless softly. "Because I know that we are going to leave the Institute. All of us. And soon."

"How do you know?" said Soapdish impatiently. "How *can* you know?"

Little Fearless looked at Stargazer and Stargazer looked back at her, then lowered her eyes.

"Because Stargazer has seen it," said Little Fearless.

"That stupid kid!" burst out Soapdish. "She doesn't know anything!"

"That's not true," said Little Fearless. "When she looks at the stars, sometimes she has dreams and visions, and sometimes – often – they come true."

Most of the girls had dreams, usually of the time when they were real girls with real names, but Stargazer's dreams were different. They were unusually vivid and sometimes terrifying, and there were those who believed she experienced visions and possessed the power of prophecy.

Soapdish snorted with disdain, but Beauty and Tattle stared at Stargazer, as if challenging her.

"I do see things," muttered Stargazer.

"In dreams? Do you mean in dreams?" said Beauty haughtily. "So much happens in dreams that sometimes some of it is bound to come true, by accident. It doesn't mean a thing."

"Not really dreams," said Stargazer. "They're more like daydreams. They can happen at any time, and not just during the night."

"Is it like watching the vidscreen?" said Tattle.

There was just one vidscreen at the Institute, heavily censored. On Sundays the girls were required to assemble in the meeting hall for an hour before the Gathering to watch uplifting speeches by the City Boss and sermons by the priests about the greatness and goodness of Eidolon. The X girls had the privilege of watching the vidscreen in the evenings, and were allowed to see some of the more inoffensive game shows and simple dramas that filled the schedules between the endless advertisements and political announcements.

"No. Because it isn't out there; it isn't in the world. It's pictures in my head. I can't exactly describe it. It's like thoughts and imaginings, only different. More real, and yet not quite completely real, and yet not make-believe either. Sometimes I see the future, other times just a possible future that may or may not happen. The pictures come at the strangest times – perhaps when I'm ironing the clothes at the laundry and I've burnt myself on the hot metal, and am thinking only of the pain. Then suddenly the pain might disappear and these pictures come, these … these…"

"Visions," said Little Fearless.

Tattle snorted. She had heard these stories about Stargazer's special powers before, and she didn't believe a word of them.

"Can't you see she's telling the truth?" said Little Fearless angrily. "Are you like the people in the City who can't tell the difference between truth and lies?"

"Perhaps it's true," said Soapdish quietly.

Tattle turned her head away in disgust. "I'm not listening to someone who's spent most of her life in a loony bin."

It was true that Stargazer, who was an orphan – her parents had been killed by a terrorist bomb when she was a toddler – had been brought to the Institute from a psych zone. Only Tattle was tactless enough ever to mention it. Many of the girls in the Institute were ill, or disturbed, and were stuck with being labelled mindcrips. They had been sent to the Institute not because they had committed any crime but because it was feared that sooner or later they might. This was what had happened to Stargazer, who had been branded insane after she had insisted that her visions were real.

"Tell them about the end of the Institute," urged Little Fearless, ignoring Tattle.

"I saw strange things only two nights ago," began Stargazer. "I was awake and looking at the stars, after all the other girls were asleep. As I was watching them, the stars began to dance. I thought I was going crazy, and I was scared, but they formed themselves into pictures and some I could understand and some I could not, but I could not tear my eyes away because the pictures were soaked with meaning and full of tomorrows.

"Some of the stars became people, great crowds of angry people, standing outside the Institute and shouting – but I couldn't make out what they were shouting. And then they dissolved, and suddenly I could see the Institute as if from outside, with its cosy walls and ivy leaves, instead of black metal and barbed wire, but the camouflage began peeling away like the skin of paint on wood when it has been burnt. And as I watched, the gates burst open and the crowds came in like a vast wave. And I saw the Controller, his head hung low, his spirit broken.

"Then the pictures changed again. Suddenly I saw all the girls. They were rushing to meet the crowds. Although I did not count them, somehow I knew there were exactly nine hundred and ninety-nine. One girl was missing.

"Then I saw the walls of the Institute fall, and the buildings razed to the ground, and there were flames and cries, and suddenly all that vanished and there was simply a girl – no, the *shadow* of a girl – alone on the ground. And the girl, the girl who was missing, the girl who turned into a shadow, her name … her name…"

At that moment, two things happened. Stargazer fainted; and at the end of the alleyway a figure appeared.

It was Stench, the keeper of the rubbish dumps.

Stench marched down the narrow alley, the five girls in the sights of her small, scrunched-up eyes. She was short and wide and as powerfully built as a sumo wrestler, and her uniform was slightly too small, so she seemed to bulge all over the place without being quite able to get out, like an idea trying to escape from her shuttered, closed-in mind.

Stench was an odd creature. She was far from being the

cruellest of the X girls, but she was definitely the biggest, certainly the strongest and quite possibly the stupidest. The strangest thing about her was that although she had landed the job that every X girl wanted to avoid more than any other – that of overseeing the stinking mountains of the rubbish tips – Stench seemed to love her job. She viewed the rubbish as her kingdom, the one thing she could call her own, and she patrolled it and tidied it, and kept it in order as if it were a delicate flower garden. It was said that Stench was always rooting through the rubbish because she believed that one day she would find something precious among the rotting food and broken furniture and empty bottles and cans. She was a pathetic creature, her dull spirit surviving somehow on impossible dreams and hopeless hopes, and many of the Y and Z girls felt sorry for her rather than hating her like they did most of the X girls.

But Little Fearless and her friends didn't feel sorry for her right then, as she charged down the alley towards them, her shadow a great dark stain spread by her advancing bulk. Little Fearless was concentrating on bringing Stargazer back to her senses by patting her on her cheeks, shaking her gently and whispering in her ear. The other girls, even Tattle, were struck dumb as if they were stranded in the path of a charging rhino.

"Stand up!" bellowed Stench. She seemed to have only two volume levels, loud and very loud, and this was in the second category. Immediately the three Y girls rose to their feet. Little Fearless was still trying to rouse Stargazer.

"You deaf?" yelled Stench, fixing her gaze on Little Fearless, who had Stargazer's head cradled in her arms.

Little Fearless looked up at her, unintimidated. When she spoke, she spoke mildly and politely, without a trace of nervousness.

"We're sorry. But Z242 here is not well. She's very weak and sensitive, and was so overcome by the beautiful smell from the rubbish that she fainted."

Soapdish, Tattle and Beauty all glared at Little Fearless. She was mad to provoke Stench further by making fun of her kingdom of rubbish.

But Stench blinked twice and looked puzzled. "What are you talking about?" she snapped. "Are you making fun of me?"

"Not at all," replied Little Fearless quietly. "Why do you think we were here in the first place? We came because Z242 told us about the scent, and we wanted to smell it too."

Although Stench was stupid, she wasn't stupid enough to believe that any of the other girls in the Institute felt the same as she did about the rubbish dumps. Although it was true that she had come to love the aroma of rotting food, she knew everyone else found it repulsive.

"Get up on your feet! You're talking nonsense. You think it stinks here, like everyone else. You're making fun of me, and I'm going to make sure that you regret it."

Stargazer was beginning to come round. Little Fearless gently massaged her temples.

"You don't understand. It's not the garbage we've come to smell. No, Stargazer told us there's a secret hidden underneath all the smell of decay and rottenness, and that it's beautiful, and she brought us here because she wanted us to smell it too."

Tattle, Soapdish and Beauty didn't have a clue what Little Fearless was talking about, but, sensing Stench's gaze on them, they nodded hesitantly as if in agreement.

"She has special powers. She can see what others don't see, and sense what others don't sense. She claims that here, right at the heart of all the rubbish, there is something precious, and that she can actually smell it, and it has a scent that is both wild and rich."

To the surprise of Tattle, Soapdish and Beauty, Stench nodded, and when she spoke again her voice was softer, less angry.

"Is she the one they call Stargazer?" she asked, at almost a normal volume.

"She is," said Little Fearless. "Could we have some of your water to help her come to her senses?"

To the amazement of the others, Stench reached for her belt where she kept her water bottle and passed it to Little Fearless, who splashed some onto Stargazer's face. Stargazer shook her head and her eyes flickered open.

"She's right," said Stench, helping Stargazer to her feet. "There *is* something precious here. I've been searching for it all these years I've been looking after the tips, and I can also smell it sometimes. It's as if I have a sixth sense, like her."

Tattle nervously choked back a laugh. Immediately Stench turned on her, grabbing her arm roughly so that she could see her steel identification bracelet.

"Y558. I've heard about you. You talk too much, everybody says. Think you're a hard case but you're as soft as muck. You need shutting up. You can talk all you want in the Discipline Block, only there's no one to listen. Except for the rats, of course."

Just then, Stargazer let out a low moan. "The shadow," she said, staring ahead of her but not seeming to see anything. "It's you."

"What is she talking about?" asked Stench nervously.

Hearing her voice, Stargazer turned to Stench. Immediately her face softened, and to everyone's amazement she reached out and touched Stench softly on the arm.

"Thank you. Thank you, Lila. You are good. You are good."

Stench looked like she'd been slapped. "What did you call me?" she gasped, taking a step backwards.

"Lila," said Stargazer in a quiet, firm voice. "You are Lila."

Stench looked around her, bewildered. She jerked her arm away from Stargazer's touch and chewed at the air as if she could find no words. Then she withdrew a step.

"Get back to your hall in the Living Block. All of you. And don't let me catch you here again, otherwise I'll report you. The Controller won't stand for it. You'll go to the Discipline Block. Get away. Get away from here before I change my mind."

Stargazer rose unsteadily to her feet, helped by Little Fearless, and the five girls started to walk as briskly as they could away from Stench. The X girl stayed rooted to the spot and did not speak again.

Stench

*Anyone attempting to escape the
protection of the school shall suffer
the severest punishment under
City penal law, as shall anyone
(a) aiding that person; (b) withholding
knowledge of any escape attempt.
Furthermore, all the residents of the
school shall be punished in the event
of any such attempt being made.*

Rule 1, *Book of Regulations*, City
Community Faith School for Retraining, Opportunity and Hope

It was a few days after the incident in the alley that Little Fearless realized she had to escape.

She had to be loyal to her dead mother; she had to be brave and true to herself – and that meant getting out of the Institute somehow, to tell the world the terrible secret of what was happening in there.

No one had ever escaped from the Institute before, but, inspired by Stargazer's vision of the future, she had gnawed at the idea like a terrier. However elusive the solution seemed at first, she would not let it go. She wrestled with the image of Stench and Stargazer's meeting time and time again, as if sensing it might hold some kind of key to getting out of the place. Then, at last, she had woken up in the night with the outline of a plan, all laid out in her dreams.

She debated with herself whether she should tell any of her friends. If they didn't know anything, they couldn't tell anyone. Tattle in particular had a loose tongue and loved to gossip. Soapdish would hate the idea because it involved breaking one of the most serious rules in the Institute. But she had to tell someone or she would burst, and she couldn't tell one of her friends and not the others. It would be hurtful and unfair.

So, one night, after work in the laundry had finished, Little Fearless met Tattle, Beauty, Soapdish and Stargazer in their dormitory to tell them her intention of escaping.

"There are only two ways out of this place," she announced. "There's the laundry vans, which come and go twice a day. On the way out, of course, they are inspected very carefully. I'd never make it out in one of those."

"What's the other way?" asked Tattle.

"The rubbish lorry."

"You're going to sneak out in the rubbish lorry?" said Beauty.

"That's right. It's obvious."

The other girls were disappointed. No one had escaped in the rubbish lorry before. Stench watched the bins like a hawk. It couldn't be *that* easy. Perhaps, although Little Fearless was brave, she wasn't really all that clever, they thought dejectedly.

"But what if they catch you? You'll be taken away. We'll never see you again," worried Stargazer.

"They won't catch me because there won't be any inspection."

"How do you know? Stench is very proud of her job.

Fanatical about it, in fact. No one could ever sneak out under her nose."

"I know. If she inspects the rubbish properly, as she always does, I dare say she's sure to find me."

"Well then," said Beauty. "I don't see how—"

But Little Fearless held up her hand and winked. "The thing is, *if* she inspects the rubbish. The *if* is the thing. The *if* is the plan."

Soapdish looked puzzled and irritated at the same time. "Of course she'll inspect the rubbish," she snapped. "Stench is devoted to her rubbish, and no one can get anywhere near the bins, let alone the rubbish lorry, without her knowing. She'll turn you over to the Controller without a second thought, and probably thrash you with her leather strap for good measure."

Now Beauty chimed in. "I agree with Soapdish. Have you been inhaling cleaning fluid, LF? I admit that what you are suggesting is very brave. But I just can't see how it would work. Even if you could get out of the Institute, there's a bed check every night at midnight, and if you weren't there the alarm would be raised. You wouldn't even have time to do anything useful before they found out you were missing."

"And what would you *do* anyway?" asked Tattle. "I mean, we all agree you've got a lot of guts. But what's your plan – to run around the City shouting 'Come and save us, come and save us'? They'd think you were a lunatic. They'd be right, too."

Little Fearless had expected something like this. She raised herself to her full height. Her face, as usual, was dirty and her clothes were ragged. All Y and Z girls wore clothes donated by charity shops in the City, and they were tattered and ill-fitting.

"Your families are still out there somewhere," she said in a plain, matter-of-fact voice. "When I get to the City I'm going to find them. And you have to trust me. I will escape. My plan is just too good to fail." She adjusted her old purple beret so it was arranged in a jaunty angle on her head.

"I'll tell them what is going on in the Institute. Then they'll tell others and they'll start a riot and come and raze this place to the ground. Then you'll be able to take back your real names, and become real girls again."

Tattle and Beauty looked sceptical.

"Or not," said Tattle. "Perhaps they won't believe you."

"Or worse," added Beauty bitterly. "Perhaps they won't even care."

Little Fearless was taken aback. She expected to hear that kind of sourness from the Controller, but not from her friends.

But Soapdish, surprisingly, since she hated breaches of the rules more than anyone, seemed suddenly excited. "If you really could get out…" she said breathlessly, staring at Little Fearless with glittering eyes. "I don't know what stories they've told our parents about us, but I do know that as soon as they recognize them as lies, they'll come and get us."

"I believe that too," replied Little Fearless. "But first we have to decide whose parents I go to. I'll only manage to make it to one home. One of you needs to tell me where your parents live."

She turned to Beauty and spoke earnestly to her. "Beauty. Your family is rich. You told me once that your father was high up in one of the Ten Corporations. If I could find your parents, they'd be powerful enough to help us."

Beauty avoided Little Fearless's gaze and raised her chin slightly. "My parents couldn't care less. They put me in here in the first place. Said I brought shame on the family. So they got rid of me."

"But even so…"

"What's more, I don't care about them. They mean nothing to me," she said bitterly. "They wouldn't help you anyway. They'd kick you down the stairs and call the police."

"Beauty, I'm sure that's not true. All parents love their children."

"I hate my parents, and I don't want anything to do with them, and I don't want you to have anything to do with them either, because they'll just make trouble for us all." She crossed her arms and turned away.

It was Tattle who spoke up then. "Little Fearless, go to my father first. You can tell him everything. And he'll be able to do something."

"How will he be able to do something?" asked Beauty wearily.

"He's a policeman."

"A policeman?" echoed Beauty and Soapdish together, incredulously.

Tattle flushed. She had always made the most of her reputation as a juvie, and she clearly believed that having a policeman for a father – instead of a villain or some kind of rebel – was faintly embarrassing.

"Yes, a policeman," she admitted meekly. "And I'm sure the only reason he's done nothing to come and get me is because he believes in the City Boss and the Ten Corporations. He thinks that as long as he does what he's told, the City authorities will run things for the common good of everyone. He really believes having me in here is for the best, and if they say I am being well schooled and looked after, then he's bound to believe it's true.

"But once he sees you and you tell him the real story, he'll see how he's been lied to. Then he'll be able to go to the chief policeman, who will have the power to tear this place down and lock the Controller up for good."

With Little Fearless, Stargazer, Soapdish and Tattle all now eager to put the plan into effect, Beauty began to become infected with their enthusiasm.

"Maybe you're right," said Beauty. "Maybe, since he's a policeman, he really could do something. If only you could escape. Surely no one would stand for it once they knew what was happening here, least of all a policeman."

"But why should he believe you?" said Tattle, a sudden

doubt creeping into her voice. "All he'll see is a ragamuffin little girl, covered in filth, who could be anyone. He might arrest you, or throw you out. My father was always very, very strict. He believes law and order and respect are the most important things of all."

"I've thought about that," said Little Fearless. "Give me a lock of your hair. I'll show it to him, and he'll know who I am and that I'm telling the truth. Any father will know his daughter's own hair."

Without pausing to reply, Tattle reached for a rusty pair of scissors that she kept beside her bed. She hacked off a clump of her honey-coloured hair and thrust it into Little Fearless's hands.

"Look after it, Little Fearless. When my father sees it he'll know for sure that it is mine and that I'm trying to send a message to him."

"One more thing," said Little Fearless softly. "You need to tell me your real name."

The girls were silent. It was taboo.

Nevertheless, Tattle leaned over to Little Fearless and whispered in her ear. Little Fearless nodded and kissed Tattle delicately on the cheek. "It's settled then," she said firmly, wrapping the lock of hair carefully in a piece of old newspaper. "The next time the rubbish lorry comes, I will make my escape. And I promise you something else – I'll be back in my bed by midnight so that you won't all be punished; they'll never know I was gone in the first place."

"But how will you manage that?" asked Beauty, screwing up her face in puzzlement.

"And how are you going to deal with Stench?" chimed in Soapdish. "She's stupid, but she's tough and hard-working too."

"Don't worry," said Little Fearless quietly, rubbing her temples with her thumbs as if to stimulate brilliant ideas. The thumbs left black marks, making her face grubbier than ever. "I've got it all worked out. Because Stench isn't only stupid. She's greedy too. And that's the key."

It was surprising how much rubbish a thousand girls could generate, even when they possessed very little to throw away. By the time the rubbish collection came round, the tips would resemble a small range of foul-smelling hills and valleys.

All Little Fearless did for the first part of her plan was to go and stand by these rubbish tips with a smile on her face. She wore a tattered suit of old brown tweed, the trousers far too wide and long, tied at the waist with a piece of string, and a blouse with a pastel flower pattern that looked like it belonged to an old lady from another time in history. As ever, she wore her battered beret on her head, tendrils of red hair snaking out from under the rim.

It's not easy to keep a smile on your face when it smells so badly you want to throw up, but for Little Fearless's plan to work it had to be done. She stood there smiling and skipping, and generally looking delighted to be part of one of the foulest landscapes imaginable.

Stench, having spotted her, stopped searching among the rubbish for precious things and marched right up to where Little Fearless was standing. The X girl smelled so badly that it was hard for Little Fearless to keep on smiling. But she managed a grin, although it was rigid and would not have convinced anyone who wasn't as insensitive as Stench.

"What are you doing here? What are you so happy about? You should be in your dormitory," she snapped.

"Oh, please," said Little Fearless in the sweetest voice she could manage, "I hope you don't mind. But I just thought it was so … I don't know. Special."

Stench's eyes narrowed with suspicion. "What's your number? You look familiar. There are so many girls in this place, I can't keep track. Can't remember faces. Never could. But I've seen you recently, I'm sure of it. Weren't you here with that weird one – Moonwatcher, or whatever she's called?"

"Yes, that was me," said Little Fearless. "Her name's Stargazer."

"I remember," said Stench. "She knew about the precious things. And she knew my name."

She fell silent, as if trying to remember something Little Fearless had said. "Special. What's special?" she said finally.

"The rubbish tips," said Little Fearless.

"Huh," said Stench, scanning the pile of rubbish and

scraps in front of her. But she made no move to march Little Fearless back to the Living Block.

"You don't mind me looking, do you, X12?" asked Little Fearless.

"How do you know my number?" snapped back Stench.

"Everybody knows your number. You're famous among all the Y and Z girls for being the queen of the hills and valleys of the rubbish tips."

Stench frowned, wrinkling the brow on her big football head. "They laugh at me, I expect," she muttered.

"Laugh?" exclaimed Little Fearless. "They don't *laugh*. Why would anyone laugh? They're jealous. To be the ruler of this place makes you the most fortunate girl here. You must be very well thought of to be given such a job by the Controller."

Stench couldn't help but look rather pleased at this. "Is that so? Well, I suppose … yes, of course," she agreed, for want of anything better to say. She couldn't ever remember being paid a compliment before, and she liked it. "It has its moments, I suppose. You never quite know what you're going to find."

"It must be like going on a treasure hunt every day of the week," said Little Fearless excitedly.

"Yes," said Stench flatly. "I suppose it is." Then she looked out over the expanse of rubbish and a shadow seemed to pass across her features.

"X12. What on the earth is the matter?"

"What do you mean?"

"You don't look as happy as someone as lucky as you ought to look."

Stench's face crumbled a little more. "I sometimes just don't know how I'm ever going to find them," she said, her voice suddenly quiet and wretched with self-pity.

Little Fearless arranged her face into a picture of sympathy. "What?" she asked. "What are you trying to find?"

"The precious things. The precious things I know are there somewhere."

"Oh yes, they are there all right," said Little Fearless brightly. "I'm sure of it."

Again Stench went blank, like a radio with a faulty reception. After about twenty seconds she spoke again.

"I saw on the vidscreen once, this thing. A device. It's amazing. It uses radio waves, or magnetism or something. Anyway, you just point it at a pile of stuff – rocks, sand, paper, whatever you like – and it beeps when it finds metal. It's perfect for finding treasure in rubbish tips. I could get rich very quickly. Then who knows – maybe I could get out of this place and find my family."

Stench went quiet again, this time for even longer.

Eventually Little Fearless felt she ought to interrupt the silence. "I understand," she said softly. "And I can help you."

"What do you mean?" wondered Stench, unused to anyone understanding why she wanted the Device. All the other X girls laughed at her for wanting it, doubtless because they knew there was nothing whatsoever of value in the rubbish tips.

"I can steal the Device for you."

"Steal?" said Stench, looking thoroughly surprised. "Steal from where? From who? And how?"

"I can steal it from the City."

Now Stench looked sceptical. "The City!" she snorted contemptuously. "No one's allowed into the City. Not even Lady Luck."

"I know," said Little Fearless, winking. "But you see, the girl who had this job before you – well, do you ever wonder what happened to her?"

Stench shook her head. She couldn't remember a time when she hadn't been queen of the rubbish tips.

"She left the Institute and went to join her family, and now she lives in the Sunlands."

"How," said Stench, "could such a thing be possible?"

At this, Little Fearless lowered her voice still further and put her mouth close to Stench's ear.

"Bribes," she whispered. "She offered the Controller all the precious things she found in the rubbish."

Stench frowned. *Of course,* she thought to herself. The Controller would be someone you could bribe. Anyone could be bought, that was for sure, if the price was right. But one thing still puzzled her.

"How did she find the precious things?"

"That's what I'm trying to tell you! I stole the Device for

her. I'm the best thief at the Institute. I'm the seventh daughter of the seventh daughter of an old family of thieves. I'm as fast as lightning and as quiet as a cat. No one ever catches me. The X girl who looked after the rubbish before you, X … um … 45, sent me to the City to steal for her. With just one visit, I got her the Device. Then she was able to find all the treasure hidden in the rubbish tips. Before she knew it, she had enough booty to bribe the Controller and head off to find her family."

When she heard this, Stench's voice grew low and crafty. "But how did you do it? No one can go into the City. If the Controller found out…" She rolled her eyes in anxiety at the thought.

"He won't. X45 hid me in the rubbish bins. Like you now, she was the only one responsible for checking them. No one else would ever check them, they stink so badly."

"You get used to it," said Stench, slightly offended. But Little Fearless ignored her.

"I got back before midnight. So no one ever knew that I had gone."

Stench was silent. Two little shadows flickering inside her, fear and greed, fought briefly with each other. Then she looked at Little Fearless cautiously.

"How do I know you're telling the truth? You're only a Z, even if you did use to be a Y, and so you're not to be trusted. Apart from which, you've already admitted that you're a thief, which means you're probably a liar too."

Little Fearless had thought of this. It brought her to the most painful part of her plan.

She reached under her soiled tweed jacket and brought out the bronze picture frame that held a photo of her grandparents, one of the three most precious treasures in the world to her. With a heart that felt like it was now beating more slowly and sadly than ever before, she held it out to Stench.

"This was a gift to me from X45 after I helped her. She found it under the rubbish mountains using the Device and gave it to me after the Controller had agreed to let her go home to her family. I want you to have it as my token of good faith," she said, fighting back a tear as Stench wrenched the frame out of her hand.

Even Stench could see that it was a beautiful frame and worth a considerable amount of money. To Little Fearless the fact that it was valuable meant nothing. It was the fact that it held a photo of her grandparents that meant everything to her. Whatever Stench made of it, she was clearly impressed. She thrust it into the pocket of her jacket. Again she thought and thought, which, since she was stupid, took a long time.

Then suddenly her face took on a sly and knowing look. "What's your game?" she asked. "What's in it for you?"

"For me?" said Little Fearless, pretending to look bewildered. "Why nothing, nothing at all."

"Come on. I'm not dumb, you know."

Little Fearless let her face look suddenly crestfallen. "It's true. There's no fooling you, is there? That's why you're an X and I'm just a Z. Yes, there *is* something I want."

"I'm listening," said Stench, tapping her foot impatiently.

"I want... I want... I want your job when you're gone. I want to be queen of the hills and valleys of the rubbish tips."

Now Little Fearless contrived to look very angry and resentful. "X45 promised I would get her job after she left. But I didn't. She lied to me," said Little Fearless bitterly. Then she looked up at Stench, widening her eyes – one blue, one brown – in an expression of trust and admiration. "But I know you're much better than her. I know you're honest and true. After all, when Stargazer fainted you were kind – you gave her some water. It was after you helped us that I decided I could trust you. And I know that if I steal the Device for you, you'll let me look after the rubbish tips."

Stench thought again, though by now it was giving her a slight headache. She knew very well that no one, especially not a Z girl, could ever be made keeper of the rubbish by Stench. Only the Controller and X1 – Lady Luck – decided what jobs were to be done and by whom.

Stench thought again, then decided that she certainly had to hand it to X45. She had tricked this gullible child, and she had not only got away with it, but she had got herself away from the Institute. And all for the price of an old picture frame. So there was certainly no reason why Z73 shouldn't be tricked again.

She brought her small, dull eyes to bear on Little Fearless. "Hmm," she said. "But how will you get back in again?"

Little Fearless suddenly felt confused. Try as she might, she hadn't worked out this part of her plan, although she felt sure she would come to the solution somehow. What was she to say? She'd never imagined Stench would have the wits to ask her that question. Frantically she searched for an answer.

"Come on, now. You're trying to test me again, aren't you? I'll get back in just like I did before. *Surely* you can guess how I got back in again last time," she said, desperately trying to buy some time.

"Well..." mused Stench. "I suppose it must have been in one of the laundry vans. They come into the Institute from the City every night full of dirty clothes. No one bothers to check them on the way in, only on the way out. After all, who would want to sneak *into* this place?"

"Of course," said Little Fearless, secretly breathing a sigh of relief.

"Yes, that's it," continued Stench. "The laundry collection and delivery centre is on the north side of that old square in the ancient part of the City – Angel Square. I've seen the address written on the side of the vans. That must be how you got back into the Institute."

"Angel Square! That's right, Stench! How did you work it out?"

Stench was too busy preening herself on account of her cleverness to respond.

There was one last long silence.

"But how do I know you won't simply run away?"

Little Fearless put her hands on her hips and looked up at the heavens. "Why would I run away when I could have the chance to be the queen of the hills and valleys of the rubbish tips? What in the City, with its bombs and chaos and crowds and noise, could possibly be better than that? Anyway, I came back for X45. Why wouldn't I come back for you?"

Stench had considered as carefully as she knew how. And now there was no doubt which of the two shadows fighting in her heart had won. She gave out a low, loud grunt. Which was her way of saying yes.

"As well as getting the Device, there is something else you could do," said Stench. "When you go, I want you to keep a lookout for my family."

"But how will I know what they look like?" asked Little Fearless.

Slowly, reluctantly, Stench reached into her inner jacket pocket and took out a battered old photo.

It was a glossy colour photograph, with a white border, of a family standing on a wide yellow beach. They were sun-tanned and wearing swimming costumes. At their feet were a rubber ring and a sandcastle. Behind them was a glittering blue sea. The family, a mother and a father, and a boy and a girl both about Little Fearless's age, were smiling broadly at the camera and waving, and they had their arms around one another. They looked happy and free. In the white border

77

in black pen, someone had written in beautiful copperplate handwriting *Our holiday in the Sunlands*.

"What's this?" said Little Fearless.

"My family," said Stench simply.

Little Fearless decided not to ask any more questions. She felt sure this perfect family was unlikely to be related in any way to the lumpish, unattractive girl who stood in front of her; but nevertheless she took the photograph delicately from Stench and put it in her pocket.

"Be careful with that! Keep it safe," urged Stench. She looked like she was about to cry.

"I will," said Little Fearless. "I promise."

And with that, she walked silently back to the Living Block and Hall Seven, as Stench turned once more to rummage among the rubbish.

Escape

Good words make history;
bad words make misery.

Election campaign
slogan of the City Boss

Some time later, when all the other girls were in bed, Little Fearless crept out of Hall Seven. As usual she was wearing her battered tweed suit, and in her inside pocket she carried a lock of Tattle's hair and a crude City map which she had torn out of one of the old geography books in the study area of the Work Block. Tattle's father, according to Tattle, always chose night duty because of the higher wages, which suited Little Fearless's purposes ideally.

In the fading light, she made her way carefully to the tips just as Stench was about to fill up the last of the rubbish bins. There were twenty of them, most full to the brim.

They were huge cylindrical contraptions with high metal sides and small black wheels. Even empty, the rubbish containers stank, always carrying the echo of the filth they transported. The containers were so tall, Little Fearless's head only came halfway up the sides, so she could not look into them. But she could smell them – and it was unbearable.

"Come on, Z73," hissed Stench impatiently, looking around fearfully. "The lorry comes in fifteen minutes. You must be ready."

Little Fearless got ready to climb into one of the containers. Gusts of wind swept across the rubbish tips, propelling empty tin cans along the ground. Crows picked at old scraps of food.

She was just trying to decide which container was the least awful smelling, when she heard a sound that made her scalp crawl.

It was the thin high whistle of a nursery rhyme melody. Inside her head, Little Fearless filled in the words.

The north wind doth blow,
And we shall have snow,
And what will poor robin do then?
Poor thing!

Little Fearless tried to clamber up the sides of the container nearest to her – which, unluckily, was the worst-smelling one of all – but it was too high. So Stench, beginning to panic, and using all her remarkable strength, picked Little Fearless up by the waist and threw her in. She crashed through the layers of rubbish and landed on the hard metal base with a great thud. Immediately she covered herself with any stinking rubbish she could lay her hands on, until she was invisible. The smell overwhelmed her, and she began to retch, but by sheer willpower she kept down most of the contents of her stomach and spat out the taste of bitter bile in her mouth.

Little Fearless lay very still as the whistling grew louder and louder, until finally it was right outside the rubbish container. Then she heard a voice, soft and rather musical.

"Evening, Stench," said Lady Luck, her fake-sweet voice full of mischief and spite. "And how much treasure have you found today?" She blew out a cloud of cigarette smoke into Stench's face.

The Whistler, who was accompanying Lady Luck, started to giggle moronically. Little Fearless could imagine the mocking smile on Lady Luck's face as she spoke. At that moment, Little Fearless saw a stab of light penetrating the metal side of the container. She put her eye to it. Outside, she could see Lady Luck tossing her coin up in the air.

"Please, X1, nothing at all," said Stench meekly, who, for all her strength, feared Lady Luck's power and malice.

Lady Luck smiled, her pretty face brightening, her eyes as cold as ever. "Nothing? Well, how extraordinary. What with all those valuables the girls throw away, I'm surprised you can move without falling over a treasure chest or a box of gold."

The Whistler's giggling grew louder.

"I don't think you're looking hard enough. Have you checked in there?" She indicated a box of rotten fish that Stench had been about to throw into Little Fearless's rubbish container.

But before Stench had a chance to answer, the Whistler picked up the box and pushed it into Stench's face.

"Anything in there at all? Pearls? Or a golden crown?" said Lady Luck.

When Stench took her face out, there was the remnant of a small fish head tangled in her hair. It was all Little Fearless could do, despite the danger she was in, to keep from laughing. But underneath she felt strangely sad; even though Stench was greedy and stupid, she didn't feel it was right to treat anyone like that. And Stench looked wretched and miserable.

"Well?" said Lady Luck mockingly.

"Nothing in there, X1," said Stench, choking and gagging.

"Shame. Still, keep looking, eh?" She gave a fake-friendly smile, then threw her half-smoked cigarette into the container where Little Fearless was hiding. It tumbled through the layers of rubbish and landed on her arm. She felt a stinging pain, but she bit her lip to stop herself crying out. She extinguished the cigarette with spit.

Rubbing her sore arm, Little Fearless saw the Whistler and Lady Luck walk away, giggling. Then the whistling started again. Lady Luck sang along, punctuating the words with harsh, contemptuous laughter.

"You shall have a fishy
In a little dishy,
You shall have a fishy when the boat comes in."

At last the whistling faded entirely. Then Little Fearless heard Stench's hissed voice. "You'd better bring back the Device." And with this, Stench threw the box of fish into the container. Several old bones tumbled down the pile of rubbish into Little Fearless's face.

The rubbish continued to rain down on Little Fearless as Stench tried to pack the container as densely as she could, with the worst of the rubbish she could find. There were scraps of old machinery from broken washers and dryers, shattered eggs, toenails, chicken bones, maggots, dead rats, scum from the drains – every different kind of filth you could imagine. Finally the rubbish stopped coming; then, for what seemed like ages, nothing happened. Little Fearless began to wonder if the lorry was ever going to arrive.

Then she felt herself, very slowly, begin to move. She rocked back and forth with the bumping of the container. It stopped. She heard a brief snatch of conversation. The voice that penetrated the metal walls was very familiar.

"It's cold, and I'm fed up with gate duty. Let's get this out of the way, then I can go to bed. Though I don't think I'll be able to go to sleep. My mattress is too hard. Lumpy as an elephant's arse. The hardest one there is. And my skin is quite delicate. I always get the worst shifts. Still, could be worse. Don't know how, though. Have you checked the rubbish? All secure, is it?"

"I've checked it throughly," said Stench nervously.

"*Throughly?*" said Bellyache.

"I mean, thoroughly," stumbled Stench. Inside the container, Little Fearless rolled her eyes in despair at Stench's foolish slip of the tongue. "No problems."

"Problems, don't talk to me about problems. You don't know the meaning of the word. All right, let it through. God, it stinks. My nose is very sensitive to smells. I hate..."

Little Fearless couldn't hear anything else because of the noise as the great gates of the Institute creaked open. Her container moved a little way further. Then it stopped again.

She was outside. Despite the stink and the danger she was in, she couldn't help but feel excited. She had never been outside the gates since she was a small child. Now she felt suddenly sure that she would find Tattle's father and the terrible secret of the Institute would be revealed.

She felt the whole container start to rise up in the air. Machinery on the back of the lorry was lifting her and the container up, higher and higher. She braced herself. Then the container was turned upside down, and she felt herself tumbling through the air and into the lorry. Briefly she saw a dark shape standing beside the lorry, which she assumed was the driver. She noticed in the blink of an eye that he had a small scrubby beard and a thin white scar on his cheek.

Her fall was broken by a dead cat. She burrowed down into the rubbish. The rest of the trash from the remaining containers was emptied on top of her. A small but heavy piece of rusty machinery crashed down on her head. She was stunned and felt her forehead. When she took her hand away it was stained with blood. But she didn't feel any pain. She was too excited, because the vehicle had now started to move. She was heading for the City.

The lorry rocked to and fro as it drove away from the Institute. Surprisingly, Little Fearless found herself getting used to the smell. Now a disturbing fact occurred to her. Was the battered, out-of-date map in her pocket going to be enough to help her find the police station? She could hardly remember anything about the City, let alone find her way around it.

The lorry continued at a hectic pace for about twenty minutes, and then it stopped. She heard the man with the beard and the scar get out of the cab at the front of the lorry. She heard him humming to himself, then the sound of water splashing on the ground. The man must have stopped to relieve himself by the side of the road.

Little Fearless made her way to the back of the lorry and carefully stuck her head out. There, spread out before her, in the last of the fading twilight, was the City.

Now was her chance, perhaps her only chance. If she didn't get out of the lorry now, she might be taken to somewhere so far outside the City she wouldn't be able to get back in – or worse yet, be discovered and returned to the Institute before she had a chance to find Tattle's father.

Suddenly her thoughts were rudely interrupted. The engine had started again. She held her breath, closed her eyes, flexed her muscles, and with a heave pulled herself up and over the edge. She fell to the ground with a bone-shaking thud. Just in time. The lorry shot away down the empty road into the gathering darkness.

Little Fearless opened her eyes. All around her were streets and gardens and office buildings and parks and cars and trees. She fumbled in her pocket for the map. The City was arranged logically and geometrically around seven great squares. Most main roads led into one or other of these squares, so Little Fearless, keeping her beret pulled down low, hurried down the road she was on towards the centre of the City. Once she was in a square, she should be able to find her way around easily.

But before she could reach a square, she turned a corner, and stopped suddenly.

There was a shop with a large glass window that was clean and brightly lit. Inside, there were around thirty vidscreens, all beaming out an identical image.

The image showed four members of a family. They looked familiar somehow, but Little Fearless couldn't work out why. The picture was black and white. The children went to school looking glum; the mother and the father worked, and looked tired. Little Fearless could not hear the words, but she did not need to, because at that moment, large orange words appeared on the screen: *Are you Nowhere?*

Then the screen changed. It was no longer black and white; instead there was a bright sun, and yellow sand and blue sea behind. It dawned on Little Fearless that it was remarkably similar to the photograph Stench claimed was of her family. Then, with a stab of amazement, she saw that the faces were *identical* to the faces in Stench's photograph. She blinked in astonishment. It made no sense.

She carried on watching. Instead of looking tired, the family were now playing and hugging each other. They were running in and out of the sea, and laughing, and were all perfectly brown and happy. Then the screen froze into a perfect copy of the picture Stench had given her, right down to the sandcastle and the rubber ring and the family in exactly the same pose with their arms around one another. Words appeared on the screen again, this time flashing like fairy lights: *Then be Somewhere. Come to the Sunlands, by the sky-blue sea, where nothing is black and white.* Then the picture shrank slightly, and an invisible pen wrote *Our holiday in the Sunlands* in the white border.

Little Fearless realized that the photograph Stench had given her was not a genuine photo at all, but some kind of leaflet or advert. Stench had probably found it in the rubbish and made up a story about it, then begun to believe her own story. She felt a sudden stab of sympathy for Stench – so desperate for her family that she could make up a whole history out of one saved advert.

Suddenly the commercial was interrupted by a news burst of the kind they were made to watch at the Sunday Gathering. A picture appeared of a tall, well-groomed, smartly dressed man who smiled in a grave, reassuring way as he talked directly to the camera. A caption flashed up: *City Boss insists: "Terror will be defeated at any cost."* Then the picture of the man disappeared, to be replaced with other images – people being forced into trucks at gunpoint, maps of places Little Fearless did not recognize, and people running down the street and being chased by Blackhats. There were flashes from bombs and lights in the night sky. Then another caption appeared on the screen: *Security forces closing in on Oroborous after new wave of bombings.*

Little Fearless began to wonder about Oroborous once more. Did he even exist? No one seemed to know what he looked like, and no one knew where he was. Was he evil? Or was he a hero, like the woman she once thought was her mother had claimed?

A distant clock struck eight o'clock. Little Fearless abandoned her reflections and carried on walking. After a while, she became aware of a great commotion of noise and bright lights ahead. She had hoped the road would lead her into one of the main squares; and, sure enough, she found herself in a vast square with a giant flashing neon sign in the centre that read FREEDOM SQUARE, picked out in the colours of the City flag and raised high on metal poles.

Little Fearless nearly fell backwards at the sheer intensity and pandemonium of the sight. Around the neon sign were four great shiny black obelisks with inscriptions under them. One said FREEDOM, another COMMERCE, a third PROGRESS, the last one WORK. They were illuminated by great spotlights fixed at their base. Dominating the edges of the square were more enormous signs, great banks of lights on all sides, exhibiting the flashing symbols of the Ten Corporations.

She took the tattered map out of her pocket and checked it in the flickering lights. It seemed that Tattle's father's police station was only ten minutes' walk away, to the south. Checking her silver watch, she started hurrying down the avenue that the map told her would bring her, sooner or later, to the police station. She walked fast, relieved to escape the brightness and clamour of the square.

She walked past rows of houses, each one brightly lit. In nearly all of them, whole families were gathered around enormous vidscreens watching adverts, and occasionally, between the adverts, what looked like games in which people won money, or incomprehensible sports, or half-naked singers writhing and undulating to some unheard music.

Eventually, after she had walked along about fifteen streets, turned right through an alleyway then left down a short avenue, she saw a light sticking out from a wall and, underneath the light, letters which she could just make out. They spelled out one word: POLICE.

Little Fearless felt elated – and anxious. What if Tattle's father wasn't working that night? What if he arrested her anyway, not believing her story? What if they had already discovered she was missing at the Institute and there were Blackhats out looking for her?

She glanced through the glass door of the station. There was a tall man behind the counter with a large, neutral, round face, a wide, fleshy nose and a shock of curly blondish-brown hair that was cut very short at the sides but quite long on the top and swept back from his forehead in a kind of wave. But what struck Little Fearless was his ears. Just like Tattle's, they stuck out slightly, and the lobes were wide and flabby, like purses of flesh. It was unquestionably Tattle's father.

Her anxiety evaporated, and hardly able to breathe with excitement, Little Fearless rushed up the steps and through the door.

The building had the suffocating stillness of somewhere completely deserted. There were no distant echoes of voices, no clatter of approaching or receding footsteps – none of the background static that seemed to fill every corner of the Institute. The desk behind which the policeman sat was high and stretched from wall to wall of the waiting room. Being unusually small, Little Fearless could not see over the top. Thus when she finally interrupted the soft insulation of silence, the expression on the face of the policeman was one of puzzlement.

"Excuse me," she said.

The policeman looked all around him, but could see no one. He looked up and across and behind and in front. To him the police station appeared empty.

"What's going on?" he said.

"Excuse me, please. I have some very important information."

"Information? Information? What do you know? Who told you? Who are you? Where are you? Are you from the Church? Are you from the City Boss?" The policeman sounded as if he was panicking slightly. Again he looked up and across and behind and in front. But this time he also looked down. What he saw made him frown.

He thought it vaguely resembled a young girl. But instead of looking like one of the girls in the City – who were, for the most part, neat, well fed, well behaved and had combed hair and brushed teeth – this girl, if girl it was, looked more like something that had fallen out of the back of a rubbish lorry.

Which, in fact, she had.

Her purple beret, peculiar enough in itself, was stained with grease. Her face was covered in gunk and grime, and her clothes were simply bizarre. She had remnants of food between her teeth, and tufts of matted hair sticking out from under her beret.

When he spoke again, his voice was sterner and even slightly angry. He gazed down at Little Fearless from what seemed to her to be a great height. "And who," he said, "or *what* might you be?"

Little Fearless was taken aback. Although she was used to being treated like little more than an animal at the Institute, she had always assumed that things were different in the

City, and that here people treated each other with respect and consideration.

"Please, sir," she said with a slight edge of annoyance in her voice, "I am a girl."

"A girl?" The policeman raised his eyebrows, touched his wide, fleshy nose and studied the creature in front of him very carefully. It was true – she did vaguely resemble a girl. He'd once had one of his own, and this ... thing did look more or less similar. He could see that her hands and face, under the muck, were small and delicate. And her eyes – her eyes were huge and extraordinary, one as blue as the polar ice, the other as brown as the earth on a newly turned field.

Now the girl reached into her pocket and brought out a scrunched-up piece of newspaper. She laid it on the desk in front of the policeman. He looked at it, puzzled.

"Why are you depositing rubbish here?" he said tersely. "This isn't a tip; it's an official department of the City Hall and the Ten Corporations."

"It isn't rubbish," said Little Fearless. "Open it. You'll see."

The policeman poked at the newspaper cautiously, as if worried that it might contain something noxious or even explosive. He saw that there were what appeared to be a few strands of hair sticking out, and momentarily wondered if there was a dead animal in there.

"Why don't you unfold it for me," he said wearily, glancing at his watch. It was getting late, and he really didn't want to be wasting his time dealing with every deranged ragbag that wandered in off the street.

Little Fearless, positively irritated now – had she come so far and braved such danger to be treated with such disdain? – pulled the folds of the paper apart so that the lock of Tattle's hair fell out. The policeman squinted; Tattle's hair was fair like her father's, and in poor light hard to see properly. He took out a pair of spectacles from his pocket, put them on his nose, and then prodded at the lock of hair with a pencil.

"What is this?" he said, his voice as impatient as before. "Why are you here? What do you want?"

"It's a lock of your daughter's hair," said Little Fearless quietly.

Much to her amazement, the policeman laughed. "You've gone too far now, young lady. I don't have a daughter."

"That's not true," said Little Fearless firmly. "Take the hair. Touch it. Smell it. *Look* at it. I know a father would recognize a lock of his own child's hair."

The policeman's face seemed to screw up slightly, partly with suspicion, but also with curiosity. Tentatively, and with some reluctance, he picked up the hair with his fingers and studied it through his glasses. Then he brought it close to his face, and he smelled it. He looked puzzled and angry at the same time.

"Where did you get this?" he snapped.

Now Little Fearless was confused. She had been certain

the policeman would have been amazed and excited to be brought a lock of his own daughter's hair.

"Your daughter gave it to me, of course."

Now she had the policeman's attention completely. He looked down at Little Fearless with apparent fury. "I just told you. I have no daughter."

Then Little Fearless spoke her name – Tattle's real name. And at that moment, the man's face changed. It was as if he had aged ten years in an instant. The anger dissolved, to be replaced by what looked like sadness and shame. Then he seemed to recover himself, and he looked down at her with a face blank and scrubbed of emotion.

"What is it that you want, exactly?" he asked flatly.

"I just want to tell you something. Something I'm sure you can't possibly know, but you ought to know because it is so utterly important."

The policeman took a deep breath and scratched his head. "Well, if you've got some very important information, you'd best come in," he said calmly.

And with that, he picked up the small bundle of hair and put it in his pocket, then lifted up a part of the counter in front of him that was hinged and invited Little Fearless through.

Angels

Truth. Courage. Compassion.

Monumental inscriptions
in Angel Square

Little Fearless felt flushed with hope. Now nothing could stop the truth about the Institute being revealed.

As she walked through the gap in the counter, she caught her hand on a splinter of wood and a tiny scratch appeared on her palm, leaking blood. Without noticing, the policeman led her through to the back of the station, along corridors with overhead lights that were oppressively bright, until eventually they came to a small, gloomy room in which there were only two single chairs and a rickety table. The fact that there were bars on the window did not worry Little Fearless unduly, because she assumed that all the rooms in police stations had bars on them, to stop bad people getting away. But since she wasn't a bad person, the bars were clearly not meant for her.

As she sat down she was hardly able to contain her need to speak. It was as if she sought to exhale truth like it was the very breath of her life. The policeman sat in the chair opposite, and rather theatrically took out a notebook and a pencil.

"Right," he said, shifting his weight about on the seat. "First I think you'd better tell me your name and where your home is."

"Never mind that," said Little Fearless. "I don't really have a real name, and I don't really live in a proper home. But the thing is—"

The policeman looked at her sharply. "Don't have a real name? Don't live in a proper home? Well, I don't see how you can be a proper girl at all then."

At this remark, Little Fearless suddenly felt crestfallen. She caught sight of herself in a dusty mirror on the opposite wall. What a miserable creature she looked. Perhaps she wasn't a real girl, like the policeman said.

"What about your identicard? Where's that?" he demanded.

Little Fearless blinked in the dim light. How could you have an identity card when you didn't have an identity?

"I'm sorry, but I ... I've lost it," she said weakly.

The policeman gave a deep sigh. Then he closed his notebook and put it back in his pocket. "I think you're playing a trick on me. If you can't tell me your name and address, and you haven't even got an identicard ... well, I don't see that I should waste my time listening to this so-called information about my so-called daughter." And with that, he got up as if to leave.

Little Fearless spoke very quickly. "I don't have a name. And I don't have a home. But I do ... live somewhere."

The policeman hesitated, and nodded, waiting for her to go on.

"I come from the Institute."

The policeman's face seemed to be struggling with itself. "The Institute?"

"The Institute. You know. The … the … City Community *Faith* School." She pronounced the words with a tinge of sarcasm.

It was as if a light had come on inside the policeman's head. "So you're one of those, are you?" He sat down again. "I know the place you're referring to. You're a very lucky girl to be there. The Controller is respected throughout the City for his achievements in solving the juvenile, outsider and anti-social problems. It is a good place, that's for sure. A place where you will learn discipline. Education. Training. Respect."

"But that's what I'm trying to tell you," said Little Fearless urgently. "It isn't a school or anything like it. It's a prison. A terrible place. There are rats, and we eat food that makes us ill, and everyone is given a number instead of a name, and we have to work all day long and there are no toys and hardly any books and no one is free to say what they think. Your daughter is lost and miserable."

"I have no daughter," said the policeman again, firmly.

"We are all miserable," continued Little Fearless, ignoring him. "No one in the City can know what it is really like. No one tries to come and see. We need to be saved. We need our families."

On and on Little Fearless talked. Although he was writing none of this down, the policeman nodded as if he was listening very carefully. Little Fearless talked nineteen to the dozen, and the stories poured out of her like tears. She told him how the dormitories had virtually no windows, and no heating; and how the X girls hit them with leather straps; how they could be locked in the Discipline Block for days on end; and how no one was ever allowed to leave and then when they did leave no one knew what really happened to them. The policeman carried on nodding and nodding, until Little Fearless had finally finished all that she had to say.

"That's quite a tale," he said softly.

Little Fearless almost wept with relief and gladness. "I knew you'd understand," she said, grabbing his hand. "After all, if you are part of Tattle's family – that's what we call her at the Institute because she chatters so much – then you are part of my family too."

The policeman gently removed her hand from his. He glanced down and a look of faint distaste crossed his face. Blood from the cut on Little Fearless's hand had stained his skin, colouring a patch of it crimson. He gave a shiver and stood up.

"Family? I don't know what you're talking about," he said. "Like I said, I have no daughter."

"That's not true," said Little Fearless stubbornly.

"Not a daughter, anyway, that I could call a proper

daughter," said the policeman, his voice taking on a note of disappointment and self-pity. "Not a daughter that made her father proud by behaving like a good Cityzen. Not a daughter that did anything but break the rules, stay out after curfew, say things she shouldn't, steal cars and drink narcobevs.

"Not a daughter that would allow herself to be raised properly, not a daughter that would listen to what her father said. Not a daughter that believed in Eidolon or respected him or feared him. I didn't have that daughter.

"But that's OK, because the City Boss knows how to make silk purses out of sows' ears. He knows how to make rude, difficult chatterboxes into law-abiding Cityzens who will do what they need to do so that this great society of ours can work properly."

"But you haven't been listening," said Little Fearless, anguished. "It's not a school or a place of re-education. It's a workhouse; it's slavery."

"You are a small child, and you are talking rubbish," snapped back the policeman, rising from his chair and his face flushing red. "You know nothing. You are selfish, like all children. You only know about what you want, not what is *necessary*."

"But … she's your *daughter*," said Little Fearless plaintively.

Tattle's father looked down at her, his face momentarily etched with some emotion Little Fearless couldn't make out.

It appeared first as anger, then seemed to fade into something like despair. When he spoke again, Little Fearless had to strain to hear him.

"I would have lost my job, see. The Insurgency and Antisocial Acts from the City Boss meant that parents had to be responsible for their children. And I would have lost my job, because I'm meant to be enforcing the law. Maybe I would have even gone to prison myself, and what kind of life would it have been for her then? At least now, she's having a good education, and learning about Cityzenship, and being looked after—"

Little Fearless practically shouted at him. "But it's a lie! She's not being looked after. She's treated like dirt. We all are. Can't you see? We are innocent, and you are all just looking away!"

Instead of responding, the policeman gazed stonily at Little Fearless, his lips pursed, and then suddenly he turned on his heel and walked towards the door.

"Good words make history; bad words make misery."

He shut the door after him, leaving Little Fearless alone, and returned to his desk.

It was cold in Little Fearless's cell. The room was damp, and she was exhausted and hungry. She still wasn't sure what to make of Tattle's father, or what he was going to do. Maybe what she had told him was so serious that he had to fetch other policemen to hear it, and didn't want to risk her running away.

She waited and waited, but he did not come back. After a while she drifted off to sleep. She dreamed of the Sunlands, the place she had seen in Stench's photo and then on the vid-screens in the shop. There it was never cold, and there was a shining blue sea, and families that loved one another gathered together happily on the beaches, and they all looked after each other and never let anything terrible happen.

At one point in the dream there appeared a huge ice cream van made of dull grey steel that played nursery rhymes as the children queued up to buy cones and ice lollies. There on the beach in the Sunlands, out of place because of its grim exterior, it played:

Half a pound of tuppenny rice,
Half a pound of treacle.
That's the way the money goes,
Pop! goes the weasel.

Little Fearless was in the queue getting closer and closer to the front. Soon she would have a vanilla ice cream and she would share it with her family, who were waiting for her on the beach.

Then, to her surprise, the bells of the ice cream van changed. The sound thinned and spread, until it wasn't bells at all.

It was a soft, hollow whistle.

Gradually, and with a shock, she realized that she was no

longer asleep. Her eyes were open, and she could see the walls of the cell. But somehow she could still hear the nursery rhyme. "Half a pound of tuppenny rice…" Then the song changed. Now the tune was "Pussycat, pussycat, where have you been?"

With a sinking, sickening feeling, she realized that it was the Whistler. The Whistler was in the police station. And there was another voice too – dry, scratchy, bloodless. She rushed to put her ear against the door.

"And this girl," said the voice, "what does she look like?"

"You had better come and see for yourself," responded the policeman.

Little Fearless looked around her in panic. There was no way out other than the small barred window. This prison was old and had been built for adults, so the bars seemed quite wide to the eyes of a child. And Little Fearless was very small for her age. She quickly pulled the chair over to the window and climbed up on it and tried to squeeze through.

The bars were too tight. She couldn't get out.

She pushed and pushed. It was so tight on her chest that she could hardly breathe. No good. She was stuck. She pushed and pushed, until she felt she would start to bleed.

Moments later, the Controller burst into the cell. Right behind him came the Whistler and Lady Luck, tossing her silver coin, and finally the policeman.

"Where is she?" the Controller snapped at the policeman.

"I – I – but she was here!"

The Controller whipped round, white-cheeked and narrow-eyed. "You've let her go, you stupid man." Now his voice was cold and harsh.

At that very moment, Little Fearless was listening on the other side of the window. With a final push she had managed to pop through the bars and drop to the muddy street below. She decided she didn't want to hear any more. She ran.

The Controller had previously been the picture of politeness and respect that the policeman had expected. Now he spoke to the policeman as if he were a dog.

"My colleague the City Boss will hear about this, you can be sure. I've never seen such incompetence. You are scum, man. You are worthless. A liability to the City. A waste of the Corporations' money."

The Whistler marched up to the cell window and peered out into the darkness. But Little Fearless was out of sight. She began to whistle grimly.

Wee Willie Winkie runs through the town,
Upstairs and downstairs in his nightgown,
Rapping at the window, crying through the lock,
Are the children all in bed, for now it's eight o'clock?

Lady Luck spat on the floor, caught her coin, looked at it, and shook her head.

"What did this girl look like?" barked the Controller to the policeman, who was now completely taken aback.

"Well … she was very dirty; it's very hard to say … barely like a girl at all."

"That tells us nothing, Officer. This is very important. There must have been something that might enable us to identify her."

The policeman thought about the blood on his hand and the lock of his daughter's hair. Then he thought about the girl's blue eye and her brown eye shining from her filth-encrusted face like glowing lamps of life. He thought about his own daughter, and a stab of pain and regret shot through his heart. Then he looked right into the Controller's pale, papery face and tinted spectacles.

Then he said, very firmly, "No, nothing at all."

"Nothing?"

"No. Nothing. Now I will have to bid you good evening. I have a great deal of work to do."

The Controller stared at him in a blind fury. But the policeman did not flinch.

"You haven't heard the last of this," spat the Controller. Then he turned on his heel, muttering, and stormed out. Lady Luck and the Whistler scowled and followed him.

The policeman watched them go, then let out a deep, sorrowful sigh.

Later that night, in bed, he did not sleep well at all, but dreamed of the girl with no name, reaching for him, touching him with her blood, and asking for help; and of his lost daughter, though he could hardly remember her face. In his hand he clutched a tiny lock of hair, all through the night, as he shifted restlessly, stumbling blindly through his dreams.

After squeezing through the bars, Little Fearless ran as fast as she could. Despite being cold and tired she ran in even, strong, determined strides. She frequently consulted the rough map that showed her the route to Angel Square, where the laundry delivery and collection depot was, fighting off panic and trying not to lose her way.

Angel Square was in the oldest part of the City. It had existed for hundreds of years, before the City Boss, before the Ten Corporations, before Freedom Square, before Eidolon became the official god of the City. In those days, there were no gods. There were only men and women who worshipped human powers, and who were not so afraid of life and death that they needed to keep busy all the time, and invent gods to make themselves feel safe and good.

Little Fearless ran down dark streets, cobbled alleys, wide avenues. She had but one thought in her mind. To get away from the Controller and the Blackhats who had surely been set on her tail by now.

It was well after eleven o'clock when she stumbled into a wide open space. The map was unclear, and she was tired. She wasn't sure where she was, but it was one of the seven squares. Unlike Freedom Square, though, there were few lights and no people. When Little Fearless looked up, with no artificial light to cloud her vision, she could see great clusters of stars glittering in the sky. Stargazer, who knew about the heavens, had once told her that they pumped out starlight and gravity in vast, everlasting waves that moved the planets and filled the universe, holding it together in an infinite, beautiful and ever-expanding web. Little Fearless felt a shiver of terror at the vastness of it all, then a ripple of ecstasy at its mystery and beauty. She suddenly felt that she wasn't outside it, looking heavenwards, but the heavens were somehow inside her. That her skin was not a barrier to everything but a bridge linking her to all that there was. All things were one thing; and all events, one event. She felt that she was part of an infinite unfolding that was complete and perfect.

The vision left her as suddenly as it had visited. She tore her eyes away from the sky and looked around. It was peaceful, and barren, and cold. There were no signs anywhere to tell her where she was. She searched the gloom for some sort of clue. Gradually she made out three unmoving shapes about fifty feet away. She walked towards them, and as she approached they became clearer. She could see a wing, a leg, and then a shoulder. Were they giant birds? Were they frozen, mutated people?

A few seconds later, she was able to make them out. Three marble angels stood in the middle of a dry fountain.

She was in Angel Square.

The angels were old and broken-down. Not angels of heaven, but the dreams of men and women, carved into stone in the vain hope that they would not be lost or forgotten. The statues were not meant to represent supernatural beings. They were emblems of the human spirit. Little Fearless imagined they had once had beautiful faces, but now their features were blurred by wind and rain, by time and neglect.

She squinted in the darkness. She could just make out the names carved on the plinth beneath them. The three angels were called Truth, Courage and Compassion. These seemed very old-fashioned words. Corny, even. Little Fearless had no time for fancy words like that. She'd have been more convinced that the angels represented something real if they had been named Doubt, Cruelty and Revenge. Or Anger, Confusion and Indifference. These seemed to be the powers that ran the world.

Nevertheless, the forgotten, crumbling angels fascinated her; but she had no time to gaze for long. She had to get back to the Institute before it was too late – before all the children were turned out of their beds and her absence was discovered. Her only hope was that the Controller would think there was no rush to bring forward the nightly inspection. After all, how was he to guess that she was going to return, having gone to all the trouble of escaping?

Her eyes scanned the edges of the square. On the north side, as Stench had promised, she saw there was a large white van, the back doors open, with the inscription CITY LAUNDRY on the side. Little Fearless saw that the van was shivering as if from the cold. The engine was on; it was ready to leave. She began to walk fast towards the van. She could make it. It was dark, and nobody could see her.

She heard a noise – another engine running close by. It made her start and look around like a skittish cat.

Twenty yards further along from the laundry van was a holiday coach, trimmed with chrome and shining clean. It was parked under the sulphurous light of the only street lamp in the square. Although the coach was empty, there were welcoming lights inside, and soft, comfortable-looking seats. The luggage hold was open, and on the front it said: TO THE SUNLANDS. Little Fearless stared. It was as if the coach itself were beckoning her. It would be simple for a small girl like her to hide in the luggage compartment and hitch a ride away from the City to a place of warmth and freedom.

She hesitated – but not for long. She couldn't stand to think of all the other girls being punished for her crime – as they surely would be if her absence was confirmed. She felt determination well up in her, remorseless, like a tide of molten rock, cooling and hardening as it rose to a crest. She ran to the laundry van. Inside, there were at least a dozen giant wicker baskets, all filled with dirty clothes from the City. She heard voices approaching, and she threw herself into the basket nearest the door and covered herself with dirty clothes.

Almost immediately, the rear doors closed and the van started to move. The smell, although nowhere near bad as the rubbish lorry, was sour and stale. Little Fearless used a soiled sweater and a rumpled shirt to try to wipe herself as clean as she could. She looked at her watch. Eleven thirty. She knew the bed check was at midnight – if the Controller hadn't got back from the police station already and turned all the girls out of their bunks.

The journey seemed to stretch the minutes out unbearably. She imagined melting clocks with snails dragging the hands. She felt sure time back at the Institute was being drawn by galloping stallions. She didn't believe she could possibly make it back before midnight, but when she finally felt the van come to a stop outside the Institute, then slowly make its way inside, it was still only ten to twelve.

Before the engine was even turned off, Little Fearless was out of the van. She closed the doors carefully behind her so no one would suspect that it had carried a stowaway. Then she ran the fifty yards in the darkness back to the Living Block, and slipped in through the door of Hall Seven. It was all shadows and cold air. She could hear two cats fighting in the distance, and the low whistle of wind mingled with the cats' cries made everything seem strange and disturbing.

As the minutes and seconds ticked away, she made it to her bunk, threw off her beret and clothes and hid them under her mattress, hoping she would be able to slip them into the laundry the next day. Her ragged pyjamas were under her pillow and, almost falling over in her hurry to get into the trousers, she pulled them on and climbed up into her bunk. She had left a damp flannel there earlier on, and she wiped her face and hands with it to get rid of the worst of the dirt. Then she closed her eyes and pretended to be asleep.

Then she heard a small, timid voice from the bunk below her. "Little Fearless?"

Stargazer was awake. Despite her gruelling work, she had not fallen asleep. Instead she had watched the stars through the tiny skylight, and waited for Little Fearless to return.

"Stargazer. Is everything all right?"

"There's something going on. There are X girls teeming all over the place."

"It'll be the bed check in a minute," said Little Fearless. "Keep quiet and pretend to be asleep or they might suspect you."

"No one would suspect me. Everyone knows I'm too much of a coward to run away."

"You're braver than you know, Stargazer. But you must be quiet now. They'll be coming any second."

Stargazer muttered something all the same, but Little Fearless couldn't make it out.

"What is it, Stargazer?"

The younger girl looked up at her. "Little Fearless … Little Fearless … are they coming, Little Fearless?" was all she said, her voice faint as dust.

"What?" said Little Fearless, hardly listening, so worried was she about the bed check. She glanced down at Stargazer's pale, frightened face.

"Our families … are they coming to get us?"

Looking at the hope in Stargazer's eyes, like a blue spark shed by her soul, Little Fearless felt sad, but didn't show it. Instead she quickly grabbed her hand, their locked bracelets glancing against one another.

"Of course they are. But I will have to go back one more time. I haven't found enough of our families yet. Not enough of them to tear down the walls of this place for ever."

"But they're coming?"

"Yes, yes," said Little Fearless, hesitating only for the smallest fraction of a second. "Of course they're coming."

Stargazer gave a broad smile. "I know, Little Fearless. I have seen it."

Then they fell silent and closed their eyes. At that exact moment, the midnight bells sounded and the dormitory doors opened.

A familiar croak sounded throughout Hall Seven. "Everybody out of their beds *immediately*." Although the Controller said the words quite softly, his voice carried to every corner of the room.

As Little Fearless pretended to yawn and stretch, she saw that the Controller had the Whistler, Lady Luck, Bellyache and Stench with him. Lady Luck was chain-smoking with one hand and tossing and catching her silver coin with the other. The Whistler was neither whistling nor giggling – instead she looked stern and angry. Bellyache was muttering to herself. As for Stench, she simply looked very nervous. When her eyes fell on Little Fearless, a look of pure terror rippled across the pale wasteland of her features.

The X girls immediately set about throwing anyone still dozing out of their beds. The children squealed in pain, shock and discomfort. Stench and Bellyache went down one side of the dormitory, the Whistler and Lady Luck the other.

Bellyache talked incessantly, as much to herself as anyone else. "What have you been up to now? Can't trust any of you. Look at the dirt under this bed. You Z letters are always so filthy. As for the Y girls – who do you think you are? Think you're special. You're not. You're worth less than what's on the sole of my shoe. Slime. Mud. Decay. Germs. Straighten up. Bend down. Get out. Get in. Stand still. Move out the way. Shut up. Speak louder."

The Whistler whistled to herself quietly between her teeth as she slapped and pinched any children who didn't move fast enough, while Lady Luck tossed her coin up and down in the air, a joyless smile fixed on her lips like a rime of frost.

The Controller looked more and more agitated as the rumpus grew and girls complained and cried. "SILENCE!" he barked finally.

A minute or two later, all the girls were standing to

attention next to their beds. Lady Luck and the rest of the X girls went up and down the lines, counting. They finished, and consulted with one another. Then Lady Luck, looking rather puzzled, marched up to the Controller.

"They're all here, Controller."

"That's impossible," he said impatiently. He grabbed Lady Luck by the shoulders and put his face up to within an inch of hers. She flinched. He spoke very softly to her, and stroked her cheek menacingly. "Count again. The checks in the other halls are finished and all the beds are occupied. Your mathematics must be inaccurate."

So they counted again. And then again. No one was missing.

The Controller turned the colour of stone. Not one of the girls could ever remember seeing him so angry. Even Lady Luck looked nervous. He marched into the centre of the ranks of beds so that all the girls could hear him clearly.

"Something very serious happened tonight," he said. "Something disgraceful. Something unforgivable."

He was silent for a long time, as if to impress on them how serious the matter was.

"Someone in the Institute escaped – I mean, left the protection of the school, and somehow found their way into the City."

At this pronouncement there was a buzz of excitement that spread around the dormitory, which the X girls immediately suppressed with a flurry of strappings and cursing.

"I want the girl who did this to have the guts to admit it. Right now."

Nobody moved. Lady Luck, however, twitched her nose and moved to within a few feet of Little Fearless. "You reek, Z73," she said. And it was true: Little Fearless bore the noxious imprint of the night's journeys on every inch of her skin. "You stink more than Stench."

Lady Luck began to look suspicious as she sniffed the air and stepped towards Little Fearless's mattress, where her dirty clothes were hidden, but the Controller stopped her.

"Never mind your obsession with personal hygiene, X1," he snapped. "We have more important matters to attend to."

Lady Luck reluctantly moved away, still glancing suspiciously at Little Fearless. When the Controller spoke again, it was to the whole dormitory.

"Each and every one of you must understand this very clearly. I will not stand for this kind of behaviour. If the individual who did this does not own up right this moment, every single Y and Z girl will be punished. This, as you know, is the first rule of the Institute." And he looked directly into the brown and blue eyes of Little Fearless, so that Little Fearless could see her own eyes reflected in his tinted glasses.

Little Fearless felt her heart begin to race. She wasn't scared of owning up. She was prepared to accept her punishment, because she always believed in taking responsibility for whatever it was she did. But she also knew that she needed to escape again. She needed to keep trying. All she had to do was find someone in the City who would listen to her.

So, with some reluctance, Little Fearless remained silent.

It then occurred to Stargazer that the brave thing for her to do would be to pretend that it was she who had run away. Then Little Fearless would not be caught and she would be able to go and get all their families, and it would save everyone from being punished. But it was just a fleeting thought. The scared part of her was still much bigger than the brave part. She knew she could never be like Little Fearless.

So the threatening silence went on and on.

When the Controller spoke again, it was more like the voice he usually used – dry, soft, insinuating.

"Come on now. I know that whoever did this could not have done it alone. They must have had help, and that help must have come from an X girl."

Little Fearless saw the colour drain from Stench's face. A blood vessel began to throb just above her right eye. There was a faint sheen of perspiration visible on her forehead.

"It is far more important to me to catch the X girl who has shown such terrible disloyalty to me personally than it is to catch some reckless, foolhardy girl who wanted an adventure. So the person who actually escaped will have a lenient punishment – compared to whoever it was from the X category who helped her. But if I find out who she was the hard way, then the punishment for the girl that escaped will be grim indeed. More severe than you can possibly imagine."

Stench seemed to be holding her breath. But Little Fearless kept her lips pinched closed.

"So be it," muttered the Controller bitterly. "You will *all* suffer the penalty, as the rules prescribe. And you won't forget it in a hurry."

With that, he abruptly left the room, which was now filled with an atmosphere of fear, shock – and just the slightest trace of hope.

The Meeting

We must be gentle, but tough as nails.
We must be kind, but cruel as winter.
We must be tolerant –
but absolutely without mercy.

The City Boss

The laundry was a single vast hall with enormous rotating washing drums, and dryers that roared hot air and raised the temperature to unbearable levels. There were intense blue-white overhead lights, which glared off shiny metallic pipes that moved the hot air for drying the clothes from place to place and had once provided some form of ventilation before the cooling mechanism had broken and never been fixed. Hundreds of Y and Z girls, watched over by ranks of X girls, laboured all day to get the clothes of the City clean.

Tattle, Soapdish, Beauty, Stargazer and Little Fearless had managed to find a corner of the laundry where no X girls were patrolling, and Tattle hissed at Little Fearless urgently over the clatter and whoosh of the machines.

"Did you find him, Little Fearless? Did you find my father?" she asked, hardly able to contain her excitement. She pulled nervously at the soft lobes of her protruding ears.

Little Fearless looked around, making sure that they couldn't be overheard. She put her arm round Tattle's shoulders.

"I found the police station, Tattle. But your father wasn't there. I'm sorry."

Immediately Tattle's face took on a bereft, crestfallen look. Her tall, rangy body slumped.

"So it was all a waste of time," said Soapdish curtly, carefully folding a newly laundered shirt in a perfect geometrical shape. "The risk, the punishment. All pointless."

"Not exactly," said Little Fearless. "I did meet a policeman, and I showed him your hair, Tattle, and I told him the story of the Institute."

"And what did he do?" asked Beauty urgently, her almond eyes hooded yet fascinated.

Little Fearless paused. She hated lying. But she also knew that sometimes it was better to tell someone you cared about a small lie, rather than a larger truth that might crush them.

"He didn't do anything. I had barely finished telling him the story, when I heard the Whistler outside the station. I don't know how they found me. But as soon as I heard her I ran – just in time."

Now Tattle's sadness seemed to curdle into irritation. "You're lying, Little Fearless. How could they know you were there? Why would they come to the station unless someone had told them?"

Little Fearless said nothing, for she had no reply.

"The policeman rang the Institute, didn't he?" finished Tattle bitterly.

Little Fearless paused, and then nodded. "I'm sorry. I didn't want to disappoint you too much. But yes. He didn't believe me."

Beauty flicked her hair back from her face, and bit her lip. "What chance is there for us? Not even a policeman will believe you."

"There may be a chance," said Little Fearless, allowing a note of hope to creep into her voice. "He seemed a good man. He was just trying to follow the rules and do what people expected of him. I simply don't think he could believe that the City Boss and the Ten Corporations, who pay his wages and are meant to look after everybody, could be capable of anything like this.

"But I don't know – I felt I left a trace of myself there somehow. That I made an impact. I could see it in his eyes. Somewhere, under the obedience and keeping-his-nose-clean, there was kindness. Yes, he called the Controller. But he was uneasy. Perhaps he'll think about it and do something. All the same, I can't rely on him."

"What do you mean?" said Stargazer nervously.

"I'm going to have to go again," said Little Fearless simply. Stargazer looked shocked and afraid.

"How can you?" asked Beauty. "The security is now tighter than ever before."

"Things will quieten down. As long as they don't replace Stench, we'll be OK. I can try again, with her help. But whose parents should I try and find next time?"

There was a long pause. Beauty looked aloof and indifferent once again. "I've told you, my parents wouldn't want to know even if you could find them. They never had any time for me. Always too busy working. Anyway, I'm finished with them."

Beauty stuck her nose in the air and looked proud and indifferent. But Soapdish spoke up, in her precise, well-modulated voice. "You could try mine. I can't remember much about them, but I remember our address. It's impossible to miss – in sector four, about three hundred yards down from one of the biggest worship zones in the City. In a row of brown and white houses."

Little Fearless nodded. "I need something that will show them I know who you are. Something familiar to them."

Soapdish took the rag doll that she carried with her at all times out of the pocket of her overalls. "My doll, Toussaint. He was a present from my parents when I was born. He's very special to me. They'll recognize him."

Little Fearless nodded. Then Soapdish produced some paper and a pencil out of her pocket. She wrote an address. She drew a picture of a small house with a pitched roof, and a few pot plants in the garden. She added windows, and the outline of people at the windows. Their faces were featureless, blank.

"Perhaps one day, with your help, I will once again know what they look like," she said.

Later that day, the punishment began. All the Y and Z girls had to have their hair cropped close so that they were nearly bald.

Little Fearless didn't think it seemed too bad. It did not involve hurting anybody, or locking anybody away. Most of the girls were relieved when they heard that a haircut was to be their only punishment. As the children queued up for the barber's chair, many of them felt quite cheerful at having got off so lightly. Some even liked the way they looked shorn and clean-headed.

But after a day or two with their new hairstyles, they didn't feel quite so cheerful.

For what they realized was that they had all begun not only to look more and more like each other, but to feel less and less like themselves. If it hadn't been for their richly varied vagabond clothes it would have been hard to tell them apart. No one looked pretty – apart from Beauty, of course – and no one looked ugly. No one looked special and no one looked ordinary. No one looked younger and no one looked older. This, they very quickly realized, made them feel empty and hollow. Not having any mothers and fathers, and not having any names, the girls sometimes doubted that they themselves were real. Now they were all indistinguishable, and even less like girls than before. It became harder than ever to believe that they were real children with real families (somewhere) and real minds and real feelings. They felt more and more like they imagined statues might feel if they were alive, or black and white pictures on a page, flat and two-dimensional.

There was another unpleasant consequence. The X girls seemed to be even crueller to them than they had been before. Most of the X girls had always been distant and unsympathetic, but there were a number of them that often weren't so bad and would help them occasionally and even talk to them almost as if they were equals. Now those girls became fewer and fewer. Little Fearless decided the reason the X girls were crueller to them was because the X girls had begun to think of them as creatures, rather than children. Vermin, or insects perhaps. After a while, it was hard for the children not to think the same thing about themselves.

This wasn't the case with Little Fearless, whose spirit seemed unbreakable. But she needed all her reserves of courage. Because, once it sank in what was going on, and how tough the punishment was, some of her friends became angry with her.

"Her and her tricks. They've backfired on all of us," said Tattle, despite the fact that Little Fearless had risked everything to find her father. She started to do imitations of Little Fearless instead of the Controller – picking her nose in exactly the way Little Fearless picked her nose, and rubbing dirt all over her face. Beauty and Soapdish giggled. When

Stargazer complained that she was being two-faced, Tattle just laughed it off. "Don't be boring, Yellow," she said. "I'm just having a joke. It cheers everyone up. Little Fearless is still one of my best friends."

"Perhaps going to the City was a big mistake," said Beauty, being brutally outspoken as usual. At least she said it to Little Fearless's face, but that didn't stop her words hurting. "Wouldn't it have been braver to own up? It's hopeless anyway. You're looking a real wreck lately, Little Fearless. Sometimes I wonder if you're really pretty enough to be my friend."

At this, Little Fearless looked hurt, and Beauty felt a pang of regret. She gave her a hug. "You *are* still one of my very best friends, though. And my hair will grow back one day."

"And you're still the prettiest girl here even without hair," said Little Fearless.

"That's true," agreed Beauty, inspecting her long, perfect fingernails.

"Maybe your stories about our families are just that – stories," said Soapdish to Little Fearless, scratching at her scalp, happy she didn't have to get her hair dirty any more but still worried about lice and dandruff. "Perhaps you should just accept things as they are, like the rest of us. At least things are orderly, and not messy and untidy. We know where we are. We know who's in charge. Things could be a lot worse."

Little Fearless nodded politely, even though she didn't agree.

Out of Little Fearless's hearing, the grumbles went on. But if any of them took place within earshot of Stargazer, she would pluck up all her courage and speak out.

"Little Fearless is the strongest and bravest of us all. The Controller is just trying to turn us against her. If he succeeds, we will lose everything. Because we will no longer have hope."

Every time she said something like this, although she wasn't always aware of it, the scared part of her became slightly smaller and the brave part grew imperceptibly larger.

A few days later, Little Fearless stood by the rubbish tips again, waiting for Stench to spot her – which she did.

She grabbed Little Fearless by the collar of her musty tweed jacket and shook her. "So there you are. The great thief. I should have told on you."

Little Fearless knew that the reason she hadn't was because then the Controller would know that Stench had helped her. But she pretended to be grateful anyway.

"Thank you. You were brave and loyal not to betray me to the Controller."

Stench let go of Little Fearless's collar and took a pace backwards. "A lot of good it did me. Where's the Device? You didn't get it, did you?"

"I'm sorry. I've brought you something else, to try and make amends. It's something else that X45 found under the rubbish with the Device." And with this, she brought out from her inside pocket the silver wristwatch which had once belonged to her father.

Stench's eyes lit up. She grabbed the watch greedily and examined it.

Little Fearless felt a lurch in her heart, as if another piece of it were being wrenched away. She felt she was giving up part of her very self with the watch. But there was nothing for it – not if she was going to return to the City.

"Nice. Super nice," said Stench, strapping it on her hefty wrist. It was too small, so she punched a crude hole in the exquisite leather with the point of the clasp, bending it in the process. Little Fearless hid her sadness and tried to seem excited.

"But what about the Device?" asked Stench again, now regarding the watch critically. "This watch is all very well and good, but it's not going to be nearly enough to get me out of here."

"The shop where I stole the Device from last time had closed down," said Little Fearless. "But I know where there is another one. It's near. I just need to go back once more."

Stench looked doubtful.

"I've done it before, X12, and I can do it again," said Little Fearless. "What can the Controller do about it? Nothing. If I'm back here on time – and I will be – nothing bad will happen."

"I don't know," muttered Stench. "What if you get found out again?"

"What if I am? You didn't get punished – only the Y and Z girls. And that wasn't so bad anyway. A haircut – big deal."

"You could squeal on me, to save yourself."

"I didn't last time. I came back, like I said I would. You've got this magnificent watch. Soon you'll have something even more precious."

Stench concentrated. Her thoughts were like struggling swimmers in a deep, swirling torrent of appetites and desires, and she fought to find a useful one. The craving for the Device swept away everything in its path. She wanted it. She had to have it. And with it, and with the treasure it would reveal, she could fill that hole in her heart where love and hope once were. She didn't want to face the truth – that there weren't enough treasures in the world to fill that dark place.

"Be here tonight," said Stench briskly. "They are coming to take the rubbish away at sunset. Just make sure you're here before that."

And with that, she marched off, sniffing the odours in the air briskly as if she were walking in a meadow in spring.

That evening, Little Fearless returned.

Since the escape, the X girls had doubled their patrols, and Stench was nervous. Her round, hefty face was filmed with sweat as she lifted Little Fearless into the container. Little Fearless burrowed down to the bottom of the rubbish. She crouched under the layers of filth and stink. This time she had the idea of tying a handkerchief over her mouth and nose to try to stem the smell, but it wasn't very effective. Still, it didn't seem as awful as last time – maybe she was just getting used to it.

Nothing happened for about half an hour. She had almost convinced herself that the rubbish lorry wasn't coming, when she heard Stench hiss. Through the echo of the metal container walls her voice sounded thin and mechanical.

"The lorry is late. It'll be here in a moment. Stay put. And stay quiet."

Then, almost immediately, Little Fearless heard another voice – an ugly, strident, whingeing voice.

"This rubbish smells disgusting. Why doesn't rubbish smell nice? Why doesn't Stench look after it properly so that it's not always rotting away? Can't she pick up the maggots and get rid of them? Look, there's a rat. Filthy things. I hate having to come over here. I get all the worst jobs. I'm cold. I'm tired. I'm fed up with everything."

It was Bellyache. Then Little Fearless heard Lady Luck's voice, sweet and menacing as usual.

"Stop complaining, X23. Things could be worse. You could be put in charge of the rubbish tips for a start. In fact, now I think about it, you'd be ideal."

Bellyache fell silent. Lady Luck continued talking as they reached the spot where Stench was standing, beside the rubbish container that concealed Little Fearless.

"But it's hard to imagine anyone doing such a fine job as old Stench. She loves her rubbish, don't you, Stench?"

"Yes, X1."

"Yes, Stench is the princess of everything rotten, broken-down and thrown away. Found anything valuable tonight, Princess?"

"No, X1."

"Look at you, lardarse. You seem very hot and sweaty. You must have been working extremely hard."

"I have, X1. It's work that makes us real people, the Controller says," said Stench, attempting an ingratiating smile.

As before, Little Fearless had a view through the hole in the container wall. She could see Lady Luck tossing her coin up and down.

There was a long silence.

"You seem nervous," observed Lady Luck, scrutinizing Stench's still-sweating face carefully.

"Nervous? Why would I be nervous?"

"I really don't know. Perhaps you're up to something. Perhaps you're trying to hide something. Perhaps you really have found something valuable."

"Oh no. I've found nothing at all."

Little Fearless could see Stench, like an idiot, staring dumbly at the container where she was hiding. She held her breath. The stupid X girl was going to give her away. She saw Lady Luck follow Stench's gaze, until it seemed that she was staring directly into Little Fearless's blue eye.

"Something's not right here. I think we should search the rubbish bins. Don't you, Bellyache?"

Bellyache looked the container up and down, and wrinkled her nose at the smell. "Well, I don't know if it's really worth it. I don't expect there's much to see; anyway, it's late and—"

Lady Luck interrupted Bellyache. "I think we – *you* – should have a look."

Little Fearless glanced around her desperately. Her eyes alighted on a sack of decaying chicken heads that was giving out a terrible smell, even though it was closed. Holding her nose, she quietly opened the sack. The smell that came out was appalling. A foul stink immediately drifted upwards and out to where the three X girls were standing.

"For the love of Eidolon, what *is* that terrible smell?" complained Lady Luck, taking a step backwards. Stench and Bellyache followed suit. "Get in there and have a look, would you, Bellyache? I still think Stench is hiding something." Lady Luck covered her nose with a handkerchief.

Bellyache looked horrified. "My clothes are all clean. I don't want to get them dirty. I don't want to smell like a rotten chicken. It's not fair. I get all the worst work. Then I'll have to have a bath. I hate baths. They make you—"

"Oh, shut up, Bellyache," snapped Lady Luck. She put away the handkerchief and started tossing her silver coin up and down again. Her eyes traced its arc. "Tell you what, you sparkling ray of sunshine. I'll give you a chance. Heads, you get in there and search it. Tails, we leave Princess Puke in peace to guard all her skanky treasure."

She threw her silver coin high into the air, only to miss it when it fell. It came to rest a few feet from where Little Fearless was hiding. To her horror, she could see that it was heads.

Lady Luck picked it up and examined it. Little Fearless braced herself. It was all over. Now she would never find anybody's family.

Lady Luck smiled sweetly – which Bellyache knew meant trouble. X1 opened her small, delicate mouth to announce the result.

Then she paused. She had another hour of patrol with Bellyache, and it was bad enough having to listen to her complain all the time in her klaxon voice without her smelling like a pile of festering poultry. And it would make her moaning even worse.

"Tails," said Lady Luck, hiding the coin from Bellyache then flipping it back in the air, and this time catching it.

"A bit of luck for a change," said Bellyache sulkily. "That's not like me. I'm never lucky. I bet it means that now I've had a bit of luck today, I'll be really unlucky tomorrow. Twice as unlucky as usual, I expect. And I'm already the unluckiest girl in the Institute."

The two X girls wandered off in the direction of the Food Block. The drone of Bellyache's voice went on and on until it disappeared. Stench and Little Fearless were alone again.

Now she heard Stench hissing to her. "The lorry's here. Get ready."

Little Fearless heard the rubbish lorry drawing up outside the Institute. As before, she felt the container being wheeled towards the gates, then a bump as it passed through the entrance, where it was raised and emptied. She tumbled out, her fall broken this time by a rancid mattress. Her journey to the City had begun again.

The lorry hurtled along. Poking her head out of the back, Little Fearless followed its progress as it made its way towards the City. Through scrubland and along empty roads, then the darkness began to be punctuated by lights and signs, and muttering, smoke-belching crowds of other vehicles.

Eventually Little Fearless saw a sign:

YOU ARE ABOUT TO ENTER SECTOR FOUR.
SECTOR FOUR IS SPONSORED BY THE EPSILON CORPORATION
IN PARTNERSHIP WITH THE CITY BOSS.

A few minutes later, the lorry slowed down so suddenly that she almost lost her balance and fell. It came to a halt, and the engine was switched off. Little Fearless craned her neck and saw a large sign: BUY OMEGA GAZOIL AND GO FASTER. She saw the man with the scar and the scrubby beard vault out of his cab. She had a few seconds to make her escape while he filled up with gazo. She jumped, hit the ground, and slid immediately on a slick of gazoil, falling and soaking the leg of her trousers. She let out a cry, and thought she saw the man turn and stare. So she leaped up and fled, and soon she was away from the gazoil station and running down an ordinary street.

She was tempted to knock on the nearest door and spill out her story. Yet she didn't feel it would be very wise just to burst into somebody's home while they were watching their vidscreen to tell them a tale that they would be unlikely to believe.

She followed the map carefully, and within twenty minutes she'd found the street where Soapdish's parents lived – Enterprise Lane. It was a flat, plain road, and the dwellings were poor, run-down, and very modest in size. Scrubby trees lined the pavements. She worked her way down the street: 5, 39, 51. Soapdish's parents lived at number 73.

Then the houses simply stopped. The remainder had been demolished. Instead there was a huge refreshment zone selling hot java juice and taninine. Business people in suits that all looked the same were sitting inside, not talking but working – scribbling on paper, staring at screens and tapping at keyboards. Serving staff handed out drinks in polystyrene cups and sandwiches wrapped in plastic in return for a few credits. Little Fearless watched them, amazed at the smiles that never left their faces as they served the customers. Were they paid to grin like monkeys?

Little Fearless sat on the ground and buried her head in her hands. She didn't have a clue what to do. After a minute or two, she pulled herself together and took the map out of her pocket, to try to work out the way to Angel Square. Suddenly she heard an entirely unexpected noise: loud applause. She looked up and saw a great spire beyond the refreshment zone. She remembered what Soapdish had said about there being one of the largest worship zones in the City at the end of her road.

She followed the noise. It was coming from a large hall which was attached to a church – the Fifteenth Church of Eidolon, more precisely, which was sponsored by the Theta Corporation, according to the sign. Outside was a poster that announced:

THETA 15 WORSHIP ZONE.
THE CITY BOSS SPEAKS – TONIGHT.

Despite herself, Little Fearless could not resist peeping inside. She was curious to see what the great City Boss looked like in the flesh.

She crept in through a door with a sign on it that read FIRE DOOR: KEEP UNLOCKED. Immediately to her left, she saw a security guard with his face momentarily turned away. To her right were some dark stairs that led up to a small deserted balcony, a metal grille barring the entrance. Below the grille was a tiny gap, and Little Fearless wriggled her way underneath in order to watch the gathering unobserved.

The hall was crammed full of people, their faces turned towards the podium at the end. Up on the stage was the man

Little Fearless had seen on the vidscreen at the Institute many times – tall, perfectly groomed and with a winning yet grave smile. It was the City Boss. The expression on every face in the audience was one of respect and admiration. City flags had been hung all around the hall, their symbols of the flexed arm, the clock, the eye and the bundle of sticks lit by hidden spotlights.

The City Boss was speaking very firmly and clearly, with not a trace of doubt or uncertainty in his voice. He had a way of waving his hands around as he spoke that was hypnotic.

"Some people say things are complicated," he was saying, "but to me, and, I think, to anyone who possesses common sense, they are simple and straightforward. Any child could understand the way things are."

Little Fearless's ears pricked up at this. She was a child, so she hoped it would be possible for her to understand what it was he was going to say. She felt she knew so little about the world that she was eager to learn anything she could.

"There are people who are like us. And there are people who are not. There are *many* people, in fact, who are not like us. *Too* many. Who do not share our values. Our beliefs. Our way of life. And I don't care what the airy-fairies and the artsy-fartsies and the wishy-washies say. They are not even people in the same way we are people. For they are not Eidolon's people."

At this comment, which Little Fearless thought was extra-ordinarily ignorant, the audience erupted with shouts of approval. Why on earth aren't they laughing at him? thought Little Fearless. How can people be anything other than people?

"Of course, I am all for toleration. For moderation. For integration. For modernization," continued the City Boss.

Many in the audience now muttered approvingly: "Hear! Hear!" and "Quite right."

"We would not be good people if we did not believe these things. However, the trouble with people like us is that people like *them*" – he pronounced "them" very sharply, as if it were a word that could cut flesh – "think we are a soft touch. *Because* we are good. So they try and take advantage of us. They try and sneak into our City so they can take our jobs, and then when they don't have jobs, they try and take our charity. And if they can't take either – or sometimes, even if they take both – they try and blow us up with their bombs in the name of Ormazd.

"Well, I for one have decided that I have been quite understanding enough for quite long enough!"

A roar of approval. Little Fearless felt very puzzled. How could anyone be too understanding? To not understand is simply to be ignorant, she thought.

"We must do something soon, or these people who are not people like us will breed and multiply and take us over completely. Then they will do to *us* what we have no choice but to start doing to *them* in order to stop *them* doing it to *us*."

The audience seemed a bit baffled by this, and only a few scattered cheers went up. The City Boss grinned broadly nevertheless. Then Little Fearless noticed a hand go up in the audience. The man to whom the hand belonged stood up. He was wearing a uniform and looked puzzled and sad. To her amazement, she saw it was Tattle's father.

"I see I have a questioner," said the City Boss. "Excellent. Ah, a member of our fine and loyal police service. What is it, Officer?"

"I was just wondering," said the policeman, rather nervously. "I'm a bit confused. If we do bad things to the bad people before they do it to us, well ... won't we be just as bad as the bad people we are trying to stop, even though we are good?"

There was silence, then a few isolated boos. One man shouted out, "Good words make history; bad words make misery!" Some began to mutter about traitors and airy-fairies and wishy-washies.

The City Boss spoke, his voice calm, measured and reasonable. "A very interesting question, Officer. The point you seem to be – very understandably – missing is that we would not *have* to behave in what looks like a bad way if the bad people hadn't forced us to stop being good by being so bad themselves."

A cheer went up. The policeman looked sad and confused, as did Little Fearless. Now the City Boss was speaking even louder than before, and punching the air with his fists.

"We must be gentle, but tough as nails. We must be kind, but cruel as winter. We must be tolerant – but absolutely without mercy."

She'd had enough of this. Little Fearless turned, scrambled under the grille and began to head back down the stairs. Suddenly she noticed a small stone corridor. There was a sign above it which read TO THE CHURCH.

The Church

*And I say unto you, go forth
and slay the unbeliever in the
name of Ormazd the Almighty.*

From the Book of Ormazd

*There is but one god who made heaven
and earth and all things, and that god
is Eidolon, lord of creation.*

From the Testament of Eidolon

The church was huge and bitterly cold. There were statues carved in wall recesses, and paintings of what the worshippers must have thought their god looked like – rather imposing and pleased with himself, like a celestial version of the City Boss. At the furthest end, behind the altar, was a small door with light showing around the edges.

Little Fearless approached the door. Behind her, in the distance, she could still hear the crowd whooping and clapping. She felt small and nervous. The last time she had come to the City, she had been so full of hope and it had all been so disappointing. She told herself firmly that this church would be different from the police station. The whole place was built out of the idea of doing good, after all.

She stopped outside the door, took a deep breath, and knocked. The knock seemed to echo around the whole church. Little Fearless waited, her heart pounding.

After what seemed like for ever, the door opened with a creak. Standing in front of her was a man in the garb of a priest. He was very old, with a face mapped with wrinkles like the dry, cracked beds of deep-cut rivers.

The priest regarded her neutrally. "And what," he said in an educated, cut-glass voice, "might you be?"

Little Fearless, slightly annoyed, answered, "I'm a girl."

"A girl, you say," he said, sounding doubtful. "You don't look like any girl I've ever seen."

"Just because you haven't seen something doesn't mean it isn't real," retorted Little Fearless crossly. "You more than *anyone* should understand that."

The priest didn't seem pleased to be told off by someone half his size with a face covered in muck and wearing a filthy, oversized tweed suit and a purple beret that kept slipping over her eyes – which, he noticed, were entirely different colours, giving her a weird, other-worldly look.

"Whatever you are, thank you for dropping in but I'm busy. I have a sermon to prepare. My duties to Eidolon must be fulfilled, and I am short of time. Good evening to you."

With that he gestured for Little Fearless to leave. But she didn't budge.

"Please. I'm sorry if I was rude; I didn't mean to upset you. I will go very soon, I promise. I just want to tell you something that is very important."

The priest took a deep breath and scratched his head. "Well, if you're a girl and you've got some very important information, you'd best come in," he said at last. "But you'll have to be quick."

Little Fearless entered the room and sat down before he had a chance to change his mind.

"First things first. Who are you and where do you live?" the priest said gravely as if he was very interested, but at the same time looking at his watch as if he wasn't very interested at all.

"I don't really have a name, and I don't really have a home," said Little Fearless. "But if you want to know where I live, it's the City Community Faith School."

At this, the priest brightened up slightly. He knew the Controller faintly. But could this really be one of his outsider girls? He sat down opposite her on the other side of his desk and looked her up and down. And frowned.

"The City Community Faith School? Then why aren't you there tucked up in bed being looked after instead of coming to me like this so late at night?"

"But that's what I want to tell you," said Little Fearless urgently. "The Institute isn't a school of any kind, but a terrible prison. There are rats, and we have to eat dreadful food, and no one is hardly allowed to talk or play, and everyone is given a number instead of a name, and…"

Little Fearless poured out all she knew about the Institute; she was so desperate to unload everything in her heart that she couldn't stop talking. All the time, the priest nodded as if listening very carefully.

After Little Fearless had finished, there was a long silence. Eventually the priest spoke.

"It just so happens that I know the Controller. He comes to this very church every now and then. He is extremely generous with our collection plate." The priest regarded Little Fearless for a moment. "To tell you the truth, I find it very difficult to believe what you tell me," he said finally.

Little Fearless immediately opened her mouth as if to speak, but the priest held his hand up to stop her.

"Everyone in the City is agreed that the Controller's school is a perfectly excellent one. Obviously something has to be done with all the, um, unfortunates and children who are, well, surplus to requirements. It is common knowledge that the school is a well-run and decent establishment."

"But *how* do you know that?" asked Little Fearless fiercely.

"How do I know it? Well … well…" said the priest, suddenly infuriated at his inability to find an answer. "I know it because … because … *everybody* knows it. And because the Controller is a respectable and decent man who believes in Eidolon and would not tell terrible lies. Unlike…" The priest fixed Little Fearless with his glare. "Unlike some little girls."

"But, sir," said Little Fearless desperately, rising to her feet in vexation. "Why would I lie? Why would I go to all the trouble of escaping just to tell you a lot of pointless fibs?"

At that moment, as she rose, Soapdish's rag doll, Toussaint, which had been concealed inside her jacket, fell onto the priest's desk. It looked forlorn and pathetic. Somehow it brought home to the priest that the pile of rags standing in front of him was not just an outsider, not just an antisocial or a juvie, but a real flesh and blood child.

And this seemed to make him even angrier.

He reached out to grab Little Fearless's arm, but she was too quick for him. With tears staining her face, she snatched at Toussaint. In her hurry, she scraped the doll against the desk and one of his button eyes fell to the floor. Ignoring it, she threw open the door, sprinted down the aisle and out of the church.

The priest immediately hurried to give chase, but at that moment, the chief priest appeared, grave and beckoning.

"You're late, Pastor. We are all meant to be meeting the City Boss after the gathering, which finished some minutes ago. Could you come and join us?"

"But—" the priest protested.

"Right away, please. The City Boss helps to fund this church, and we have to make a good impression. Anything you have to say can wait till later. In the meantime, get up to the reception room now. Praise be to Eidolon."

Without another word, the chief priest hurried away.

It was several hours before the reception for the City Boss was finished and the priest could return to his room. He yawned and checked his watch – a quarter to midnight. He pondered whether it was too late now. Then he picked up the telephone and dialled seven zeros. He was not entirely surprised when the Controller himself answered. It was well known that he allowed himself no more than three or four hours of sleep a night, so dedicated was he to the correct running of the Institute.

"City Community Faith School for Retraining, Opportunity and Hope. This is the Controller speaking."

"Controller. I'm sorry to disturb you. This is the pastor from the Fifteenth Church of Eidolon."

"How are you, Pastor? I enjoyed your sermon very much last week. To what do I owe the honour so late in the evening?"

"I thought I had better call you. Someone came to the church tonight who claimed she was from your school."

"What!" exclaimed the Controller abruptly.

"She told the most remarkable stories … terrible lies—"

"Never mind all that," interrupted the Controller impatiently. "Where is she now?"

"She … er … ran away."

The Controller exploded, calling the priest every name he could think of. The priest was shocked. He had always thought the Controller was a decent and god-fearing man, but the language he was using was very ungodly.

Right at the end of his tirade he said to the priest, "What did she call herself?"

"She didn't give her name."

And at this, the Controller became even more furious, so that it appeared to the priest that a stream of acid was pouring out of the end of the telephone.

Then the Controller asked what she looked like. The priest told him that it was hard to tell since she was so mucky and messy and ungirl-like; he was about to mention the one brown eye and the one blue eye, when he saw the grey button that had fallen off the rag doll. He picked it up and held it in his palm. He stared at it uneasily.

After all, if the Controller could treat him, a servant of the Church, with such anger and contempt, what might he do to a little girl?

"Well – what else, man?" thundered the Controller. "There must have been something that'll help me identify her."

"No," said the priest firmly, putting the button eye carefully in his pocket. "I'm afraid not, Controller. Nothing else. I can't help you, I'm afraid."

With that the Controller called the priest a dog-collared dimwit, and hung up with a bang.

That night, the priest did not sleep well, and dreamed of a soft rag doll with a missing button eye, and the sad shorn hair of a girl with no name.

After Little Fearless fled from the church, she searched for Angel Square. Eventually she found her way to the three angels, Truth, Courage and Compassion. She stared at them in all their stony, faded beauty, and realized that she didn't understand – not really, truly or deeply – the words written underneath.

Was truth what the City Boss said it was? Or was it what the Church said it was? Or was it what the Controller said it was? Or was it something held deep inside you, like a secret? What about compassion? She had looked the word up in a dog-eared dictionary when she had got back to the Institute last time. It meant "suffering with". What was so virtuous about suffering with others? There was enough suffering on one's own behalf without taking on everyone else's unhappiness too. Surely if you had true compassion, your heart would break for all the misery in the world. She understood courage, because she possessed it, but she didn't understand why she should be given the gift of it while others, like Stargazer, struggled to find it within their hearts.

Perhaps the words weren't so corny after all. Perhaps they even mattered. And yet, if they mattered, why had the people in the City allowed the angels to get so worn and faded? Why had they neglected them?

Everything was a puzzle and a mystery – not at all simple and straightforward like the City Boss had tried to pretend it was, or like the Controller said it was, Little Fearless decided.

She saw that a laundry van was parked, ready to leave. Again there was the holiday coach with TO THE SUNLANDS on the front. As before, the back of the coach was empty. But this time Little Fearless saw a driver inside, and he seemed to beckon to her, though perhaps he was just adjusting his rear-view mirror.

She took a step or two towards the coach. Surely this time her absence would be discovered. Everyone would be punished anyway, whatever she did. If there was no point in going back, well, why not head off to the Sunlands?

She took one more step towards the coach. Why wouldn't anybody believe her? It was because she was a child and they were grown-ups, and grown-ups only ever believed other grown-ups. It just wasn't fair, she thought angrily to herself. One thing Little Fearless could not bear was unfairness. And this made her hesitate. Was it fair for her to run away to the Sunlands and leave all her friends in the lurch? Sighing to herself, she knew it wouldn't be right not to return to the Institute. She couldn't abandon her friends.

She would have to suffer with them.

She stopped walking towards the coach and instead dashed towards the laundry van. Its engine had already started and Little Fearless had to run very fast. Just in time, she managed to open the back doors and throw herself in. As the van pulled away, she shut the doors behind her.

The laundry van churned and chugged along the route back to the Institute. Just before midnight, she felt the van stop again, the engine turn over, and then the van move forward much more slowly. She knew this meant she was back. Clambering over the piles of clothes, she opened the rear doors, threw herself out and sprinted across the yard to the Living Block and Hall Seven. She crept to her bunk and stripped off her clothes, which gave out a steady reek of gazoil.

As before, Stargazer was awake and waiting for her. Pale and gaunt, with her watery green eyes made all the bigger by her cropped hair, Stargazer spoke in a steady, still voice.

"Little Fearless, are they coming now?"

"What?"

"Our families … are they coming?"

Little Fearless looked down at her. "Of course they are, Stargazer. But I will have to go back one last time. I haven't found enough of our families yet. Not enough to burn down the walls and throw the Controller out into the gutter."

"But they *are* coming, aren't they?"

"Yes … yes," said Little Fearless, feeling ashamed that she had failed, and guilty that she was lying to her best friend. "Of course they're coming."

Stargazer gave a broad smile.

The door to Hall Seven swung open. In came the Controller with Lady Luck and the Whistler and Stench and Bellyache.

The beds were checked, as usual. But once again, of course, no one was missing.

This time the Controller was even more furious than before.

"Something very serious happened again tonight." His hands trembled wildly. He left a long silence so that everyone would realize just how serious it was. "Someone, despite all my warnings last time, escaped once again and went into the City."

This time the Controller didn't even bother to pretend that "escape" was the wrong word. A buzz of excitement and anxiety spread around the room.

"I have no idea, yet, how she did it. But I will find out."

Then his voice changed. It became softer, more of an appeal or a question. "Don't you understand how much harm this does to you all? I hate to punish any girl. You are like my own children; you mean the world to me. I live to make you all into good Cityzens. Dust can be turned into diamonds. Even rubbish can be useful. Surely you are all old enough to understand that society requires order and obedience to make it work properly. I'm trying to *help* you."

Little Fearless resisted the temptation to make a rude noise. But to her amazement, there *was* the sound of an insolent, defiant belch from somewhere. A tiny one – too faint for the Controller or the X girls to hear.

It was Stargazer. The belch had been the best she could do, but Little Fearless guessed that she had meant it to be louder. Little Fearless looked at her with amazement. She couldn't help but grin. Stargazer grinned back.

The Controller noticed Little Fearless and Stargazer smiling at one another and immediately pounced on them. "Do you think this is *funny*, Z73?"

"Sir. No, sir, Controller."

He glared at her, then Stargazer. Then he turned back to address all the children. His voice was thin and sharp once more. "I want the girl who did this ungrateful and wicked deed to come and stand in front of me. Right now."

Nobody moved.

"You must understand *very* clearly. I will not stand for this kind of behaviour. It is not good for anybody. It is not *acceptable*. If the individual who did this wicked thing does not come forward right this moment, every single one of you will be punished once again. And it will weigh hard on you."

And then he swivelled, and he looked directly through his tinted spectacles into the brown and blue eyes of Little Fearless. A worried murmur spread around the dormitory. Little Fearless blinked. But her mouth stayed firmly closed.

The silence went on and on. Eventually the Controller spoke again.

"As before, I am far more concerned with catching the X girl who must have helped the miscreant. And I promise that if the girl who left the Institute will tell me who it was, then I will not punish her at all. In fact … in fact…"

The Controller seemed to be searching desperately for a way of winkling out the traitor. He gave a wide and what he hoped was an unthreatening smile. "In fact, I will reward her! I will make her an X girl – and give her the job of the X girl she replaces."

Stench blanched. She was absolutely sure now that Little Fearless would give her away. After all, Stench believed that what Little Fearless wanted more than anything else was to be the queen of the rubbish tips.

But Little Fearless said nothing.

The silence built like thunder out of earshot, all vibration and threatening promises.

"So be it," said the Controller in a bitter, razor-wire voice.

The next morning, the five friends met together in the laundry toilets, which were filthy and reeked worse than the rubbish tips. They were allowed five minutes in there twice a day, and they all arranged to take their breaks at the same time. No X girls could hear them in here, but they could be interrupted at any time.

"Did you find my parents?" asked Soapdish eagerly.

Without replying, Little Fearless took the rag doll out of her pocket and handed it to Soapdish. "I'm sorry, Soapdish. I couldn't find them. And poor Toussaint's eye fell off."

Soapdish nodded, as if it was exactly what she had expected. She took Toussaint from Little Fearless and held the doll tightly to her breast. "It doesn't matter. I'm always having to sew new buttons on him. Thank you for trying. And thank you for keeping Toussaint safe. You are very brave. But I knew it was hopeless. You need to end this now," she said, placing Toussaint gently in her pocket. "You've done enough."

"Everything here is just getting worse," said Tattle. "I can't imagine what would happen if you ran away again and got caught."

"I want to try one last time," said Little Fearless flatly. "If I fail again, I will confess it all to the Controller, and so no one else will be punished."

"You *are* brave," said Soapdish. "But you're also losing your mind. Whoever you go to, they'll *never* believe you."

"If at first you don't succeed, try again," said Beauty. "But if you try again and it doesn't work, perhaps you should give up."

"But I've got a plan," said Little Fearless. "I can *prove* to anyone outside how much unhappiness there is here."

"How?" said Tattle, Beauty, Stargazer and Soapdish, all together. Their voices echoed around the dingy tiles of the toilets.

"Tears," said Little Fearless. "I need tears."

The girls looked blank.

"This is a house of nowhere. A house of misery. We have nothing here. All we have is tears. Thousands and thousands of tears. The girls cry themselves to sleep."

Little Fearless thought she heard the door to the toilets opening, and paused. But it was a door slamming elsewhere in the laundry. The clock on the wall showed that they had been in there three minutes already. But they were still alone – for the time being.

"What we have to do is collect all the tears. We'll put them in this perfume bottle that I found in some rich lady's coat in the laundry and I'll take them to the City."

She reached into her pocket and took out a small bottle

made of crystal glass, shaped like a teardrop. The label on the bottle said *Apatheia*.

"No one could ignore so many children's tears," continued Little Fearless. "So, every time you cry, every time you hear someone else cry, I want you to collect the tears and put them in this perfume bottle. Squeeze out pillowcases and handkerchiefs. Then, when it's full, I will take the bottle into the City. When they learn how wretched we are, our families will come and save us."

Tattle, Beauty and Soapdish looked doubtful.

"But who will you give the tears to?" said Stargazer.

Little Fearless turned to Beauty and fixed her with a gaze from her eerie, sorrowful eyes.

"Beauty. I know you think your parents have given up on you. But I don't believe it. They are our last chance. They're rich. If they find out what is happening, then they'll be able to do something for sure. They'll have the power to bring the Controller to his knees. Please. Can't you let me go and look for them?"

Little Fearless gazed imploringly at Beauty. But Beauty just looked more proud, obstinate and haughty than ever.

"The tears – they will believe the tears, Beauty. Don't say no, just out of pride."

Beauty looked at Little Fearless, at her filthy face and clothes. For a second, she imagined how hard it would be to try to find the courage to escape the Institute, not once, but three times.

Now the other girls were looking at her too.

"Why can't you just leave me alone?" she snapped furiously.

A door opened and a voice rang out – one of the X girls.

"Come on, you lazy dirtbags. You've been in there six minutes. Get back to work."

"Sorry, boss," said Little Fearless, briskly. "We're coming out right this minute. Stargazer has been sick and we're helping her."

"Stargazer's always sick. She's a lame duck. Just get out here. You've got one minute."

The X girl slammed the door behind her. All eyes turned back once more to Beauty.

"It's no good," said Tattle. "She's not going to do it."

"Never mind," said Soapdish, touching Little Fearless's arm. "You tried. We will always be in debt to you."

"Oh, shut up, all of you," snapped Beauty. With that she took out a pencil and a scrap of paper from her pocket, and scribbled something. Soapdish peered over her shoulder to try to see what she'd written, but Beauty squirmed away. She kept writing as they left the toilets and headed back to their machines. On the way, Beauty passed the table where they wrote out bills and letters to the customers. She lifted an envelope, slipped the piece of paper into it, and sealed it shut.

"For their eyes only," she said quietly.

"What?" said Little Fearless. The others stared.

Beauty wrote an address on the envelope then thrust it fiercely into Little Fearless's hands. "I won't let you all down. Take my parents your bottle of tears. See if they care. It won't do any good. But at least you'll have learned something about the way people are."

A Bottle of Tears

Apatheia –
because you care about yourself.

Perfume advertisement

That afternoon, all the Y and Z girls were punished again.

Instead of beating them, or locking them up, the Controller once again did something unexpected. He forced all the Y and Z girls to wear identical clothes, in the way that the X girls did. He didn't buy them new clothes, naturally. That would have cost far too much money. Instead, he took all their ragamuffin, rainbow-coloured, raggle-taggle clothes, orange and pink, blue and violet, green and dandelion, check and striped, spotted and patterned, filled the great laundry vats with grey dye, and put them all in, load after load. When they came out, they were the colour of an evening sky on a cold, rainy winter's day.

The girls didn't think this was much of a punishment. But again, they were wrong.

The Controller had started out with nine hundred and fifty girls who weren't quite sure who they were. Then he had all their hair cut off, so it was hard to tell the difference between them – which made it harder for them to believe that they were really themselves. Now, with all their hair the same length, and all their clothes the same colour, it was harder than ever. Sometimes the only way they knew each other was by the letters and numbers on their metal bracelets. So more and more they used these rather than the names they had invented for one another.

As for Little Fearless ... well, most of the Y and Z girls had guessed by now that she was the one who had escaped. And a lot of them were angry with her. She would probably have been given away very quickly, if it wasn't for one of the biggest unspoken rules – in fact, the biggest rule of all – among the girls: you didn't snitch on one another. The Controller's spies worked hard, but they couldn't find any proof. There was simply rumour. Stargazer, Soapdish, Tattle and Beauty were the only Y or Z girls who knew for certain that it was Little Fearless who had escaped. Partly to avoid suspicion falling on them, and partly because they just wanted to fit in with everyone else, Tattle, Soapdish and Beauty joined in the complaints about Little Fearless.

"She's gone and got us all in trouble again," said Tattle. "I mean, she's my friend and all. I'm not attacking her, or anything."

Then she attacked her.

"But, you know, *I* don't just go running out of the Institute every time I feel like it. I mean, I *like* Z73. But I'm more her friend than she is mine, if you get what I mean. I'm not about to *dump* her because she's done a few silly things that have made us all miserable. All the same, she needs to be shown that this has got to stop, for all our sakes. If it *was* her that escaped, of course, which I can't know for certain."

Then, by distorting her face and hunching her body up, she impersonated Little Fearless. She reached into her nose with one finger and pulled out an old muddy piece of tissue that she had hidden there earlier. It looked like an enormous piece of snot. All the girls laughed cruelly at her clever, heartless imitation.

"Why are you putting us through this, Z73?" snapped Beauty. "Everything's getting and uglier and uglier. I can't wear pretty clothes any more. When I look in the mirror it's hard even for me to tell how beautiful I am. I look just like everyone else. I look as bad as *you*. And you're a Z girl while I'm a Y girl. Sometimes I wonder why I'm your friend at all. It doesn't really work having friends with different letters."

Soapdish was very unhappy that as an incidental part of the punishment there was less of everything – food, clothes, relaxation time – and that meant there was hardly any soap, so everything was getting dirtier. She hated mess, and blamed Little Fearless for the rising tide of grime.

"Why escape and then come back again?" she complained. "All you're doing is making yourself unpopular and making us completely miserable. Next time you go, stay gone. For all our sakes."

At this, Little Fearless looked shocked. She felt she was losing her friends – all except one.

Stargazer would not hear a word against Little Fearless. If she heard anyone say anything bad, despite her shyness, she would pipe up.

"Leave Little Fearless alone. She's braver than anyone. She's worth more than all of you put together."

Time passed. Soapdish, Tattle and Beauty lost interest in the bottle of tears, so it was left to Stargazer and Little Fearless. It took twelve thousand, seven hundred and three tears to fill it. Winter had fully settled in now. The days were short, and the girls had to work by low voltage bulbs that gave out a muddy brown light. Frost rimed the flat roofs of the halls in the Living Block, and sheeted the scrubby grass in the exercise yard as indiscriminately as it did the lush green turf in the Controller's garden.

It was months since Little Fearless had last left the Institute. A few days after the bottle was filled, one Sunday afternoon, when just about everyone was beginning to forget that anyone had ever tried to escape, Little Fearless went to see Stench.

The X girl was looking quite downhearted, scrabbling among the rubbish, and she positively glared at Little Fearless when she appeared.

"Huh," said Stench, and looked away.

"What's the matter, Stench?" asked Little Fearless, sympathetically.

"What's the matter, Stench?" muttered Stench, mocking

Little Fearless's voice. "What do you *think* is the matter, brat?"

Little Fearless noticed that although Stench's words were as unpleasant as they always were, her tone was not *quite* as resentful and bitter. There was a reason for this. Stench had been amazed and relieved that Little Fearless had not given her away to the Controller, and a part of her that had not been lost, a part of her heart that had not rotted away through loneliness and neglect, even admired Little Fearless for it.

"I haven't got the faintest idea," said Little Fearless, for all Stench was doing was what she usually did and loved to do best, which was to forage among the rubbish for precious things.

"You agreed with me that there was treasure hidden in the rubbish," said Stench accusingly.

"Because there is," said Little Fearless simply. "There always is."

"Ever since I have been in charge of these tips," said Stench, "I have not found a single piece of gold, one lousy rotten credit, one stinking piece of silver of any kind."

"Of *course* you haven't found anything," said Little Fearless.

"What do you mean?"

"How could you possibly find them without the Device? X46 never found anything until she got hold of that."

Stench blinked. "I thought you said she was X45."

"Yes, yes. X45," said Little Fearless, cursing herself inwardly for her stupidity. "There's so many numbers I get confused. Anyway. Everything will change once you get hold of the Device."

"Well – where is it then?" said Stench furiously.

"Like I told you when I came back, the shop had run out. But there was a sign saying they were getting new stock in. Hundreds of them. Next time, I know I could get hold of it."

"This is a waste of time," said Stench, turning away.

"Is it?" said Little Fearless. She reached under her coat and brought out the most precious thing in the world to her.

It was the golden locket which held the picture of her real mother.

Stench's eyes lit up. She grabbed the locket and examined it. Little Fearless felt a wrench in her heart more terrible than anything she had felt before. She felt she was giving up the very last part of what was truly herself. She rarely cried. She always thought that if she started she might never stop. But now she turned away from Stench, and a tear fell from one of her eyes. The blue one. It fell to the ground next to an old discarded brown sock and a half-empty can of rat poison, and disappeared into the frozen earth.

Stench, not noticing, gave Little Fearless a smile. "Very nice."

"This is the last thing I was given by X45 in return for getting her the Device," said Little Fearless, wiping her eyes.

"Just let me try one more time to steal the Device for you. Just one more time. That's all I ask."

Stench thought, but not for very long.

The following Saturday, Little Fearless crept out of her bed and got dressed and ready to leave the Institute. It was one of the coldest nights of the year, and the wind was pitiless. She had only a few minutes to get to the rubbish tips, where Stench was waiting. In her pocket was the bottle filled with the girls' tears and the letter from Beauty to her parents.

Just as she was about to set off, she felt someone tugging at her sleeve. It was Stargazer, staring at her wildly.

"Stargazer. You must get back to your bed. You'll attract attention."

Stargazer kept hold of her. "I've got a peculiar feeling inside me, Little Fearless. I think I know why there were only nine hundred and ninety-nine girls in my vision. It was because *you* weren't there. And you weren't anywhere else either. Do you understand what I'm saying?"

Little Fearless stared at her. For one of the few times in her life she felt a stab of genuine fear. She believed in Stargazer's powers of vision and prophecy. She felt what she said about the end of the Institute was bound to come true. But she hadn't thought that it might mean the end of her own story.

"Please don't go this time," pleaded Stargazer. "I know everyone's families are out there and will come sooner or later. You've been so brave, but you can stop now. Come back to bed, Little Fearless. The wind is too cold."

Little Fearless looked at Stargazer, and glanced for a moment at her own empty bed. She had placed two pillows under the sheet in order to trick anyone who didn't look *too* closely into believing that she was in bed. She returned her gaze to Stargazer and did her best to give her a cheerful grin.

"I *have* to go, Stargazer. I have this feeling of … I don't know what to call it. What-must-be, I suppose. I don't know *how* I know I must listen to it, but I know I must be true to it, and true to the words on the locket. To be brave and to be myself. It might be dangerous, but it's the last time I shall try. Like you yourself said, you only see *possible* futures, not all of them. Besides, I owe it to all the other girls. They have lost not only their hair, and their colourful clothes, but their very names, so that they hardly know who they are any more. I have to show them that they are truly real, and that the story has an end, and this is the only way I can do it."

Stargazer shook her head sorrowfully. "But what if you don't succeed this time? I can't imagine what the Controller will do to us. I've heard the most terrible rumours. There are worse things, Little Fearless, than losing your name, your hair and your colourful clothes."

"You know, Stargazer, in a strange way, I'm not sure that that's true. Think about arithmetic."

"Arithmetic? What about it, Little Fearless?"

"He keeps subtracting from us and subtracting from us,

doesn't he? Pretty soon, even if we're still alive, there'll be nothing left of us. Nothing worth saving, anyway. We won't even be numbers any more. We'll just be zeros, like the Controller himself. One thousand zeros."

Stargazer seemed to think about this, and nodded. "I understand. But all the same, what if—"

"I won't get caught, Stargazer. Even if I do, nothing will happen to the other girls."

"How can you be sure?"

Little Fearless touched the stubble on Stargazer's head where her beautiful hair had once been. Then she kissed her, once, on the cheek.

"I can't. But it doesn't matter. Because this journey is part of *my* story, and you cannot escape your own story, because it is who you are. Knowing is not in the head. It is not thought, or explained, but felt in your bones, and your muscles and your blood and your guts. You know that as well as me. Better. I have to go now. Goodbye, Stargazer."

"But, Little Fearless..." muttered Stargazer desperately, clutching at her jacket.

Little Fearless gently shrugged her off, turned without another word and, not looking back, headed out to the rubbish dumps.

She was late for her appointment with Stench.

The moment she arrived at the rubbish tips, she guessed that something was wrong. Stench was standing there stock-still, eyes darting like a cornered fox – or perhaps a rhino at bay. As Little Fearless advanced, Stench spotted her and waved her frantically away. Immediately Little Fearless dropped out of sight behind an abandoned laundry basket. She peered gingerly round the side, praying she wouldn't be spotted.

Then she realized that the danger wasn't so much being seen as being heard. For what she saw made her want to laugh out loud.

A shape had emerged from the top of one of the rubbish containers. The shape got bigger and bigger. It was taller than it was wide, and covered in garbage, and on top of it there were layers of rotting vegetables. The shape was making a spluttering sound – and to Little Fearless's amazement she saw that it was Lady Luck, covered in filth, and coughing and spitting as if drowning in slime.

If this wasn't enough to send her into fits, another shape appeared next to Lady Luck. This one had a frayed sock hanging from one ear, several pieces of decaying cheese rind tangled in its hair and a cockroach moving at a stately pace across its forehead. It was trying to whistle, but what came out of its mouth was more like the sound of someone trying to breathe under three feet of mud. It was the Whistler.

Finally a third shape appeared: Bellyache, her enormous head covered in soup dregs.

Forlornly the three X girls climbed out of the rubbish container, almost unrecognizable under the layers of muck. Even

Stench, Little Fearless noticed, was finding it hard to stop herself smiling. The three of them stood in front of Stench, panting and retching, trying to brush themselves off but just making the mess worse.

"Nothing," said Lady Luck disgustedly.

"It was a stupid idea," moaned Bellyache. "I don't care what the spies say. No one is going to try and escape on a bitter night like this. I'm cold; I feel the cold more than most. This soup is rancid. I'll never get the smell out. I hate my job. I wish I could have a holiday. It's just not fair. I—"

Bellyache stopped talking because Lady Luck had pushed an ancient and festering bath flannel into her mouth.

"Shut up, you miserable fat fool," said Lady Luck in a voice that for once wasn't at all fake-sweet.

Then, to Little Fearless's shock, the Controller himself came round the corner. All the X girls stood to attention, which, given the state they were in, made them look even more ridiculous. The Controller came to a sudden halt and studied them through his tinted glasses, his mouth thin and angry. The smile playing around the edges of Stench's mouth suddenly disappeared, and Lady Luck and the Whistler and Bellyache didn't move a muscle. Little Fearless strained to hear what the Controller said.

"What on earth is this?" he said in a voice that held back his anger like a flimsy gate might restrain a marauding bull.

"Please, sir," mumbled X1. "We had good information

from one of our spies that someone was going to try and escape tonight. Sneak out in the rubbish bins."

Little Fearless felt furious. She had a good idea how Lady Luck had found out about the escape attempt. She was sure that Tattle had been gossiping.

"There's no excuse for appearing in public like this, covered in filth and muck. You're a disgrace to your rank. A laughing stock. I won't stand for it."

"But, sir," protested Lady Luck. "If she escapes again—"

"Escape? Escape, you stupid girl? Who would try and escape in the rubbish? Every time it leaves here, it's taken straight to the City's incinerator and set on fire! Any girl who tried to escape this way would be burnt to a crisp. That I can guarantee. You cretin."

When Little Fearless heard this, she felt the blood drain from her face. *Taken straight to the City's incinerator and set on fire!* Clearly she had been lucky that the driver had stopped on the way both times before, otherwise she would already be dead.

But what if this time she wasn't so lucky?

She waited a few more minutes, then she stared round the side of the laundry basket again. The cold wind came in mighty gusts, shaking the rubbish containers and pulling at her clothes like the claws of tiny, vicious birds. She held on to her beret and pulled her tweed jacket tighter around her. Both the X girls and the Controller had gone, leaving Stench shivering by herself. All Little Fearless could hear was the faint echo of the Whistler's sorrowful song, becoming fainter and fainter on the other side of the Living Block.

> Hark, hark,
> The dogs do bark,
> The beggars are coming to town;
> Some in rags,
> And some in jags,
> And one in a velvet gown.

It was a melancholy sound, and it almost made Little Fearless want to abandon her mission. Nevertheless, she very cautiously left her hiding place and approached Stench.

Stench looked at Little Fearless and Little Fearless looked at Stench. They both stood still. Then the tiniest flicker of a smile appeared at the corner of Stench's mouth. Little Fearless saw it, and couldn't help but smile herself. Their grins grew broader. Then they started to laugh. Once they started, they could not stop.

"Did you see X1?" cackled Little Fearless.

"Oh my," hooted Stench, holding her football head in her big red muscular hands. "The expression on the face of old Bellyache!"

"Wasn't it just brilliant when the Controller told them off?" said Little Fearless.

"Oh yes! And did you see that mess down the Whistler's trousers?"

After a while, their laughter died away.

"You know – you're not so bad for a Z girl," said Stench, regarding Little Fearless almost thoughtfully.

"Thank you," said Little Fearless. "You're not so bad for an X girl, either."

Stench paused and wrinkled her brow, as if trying to puzzle out a tricky piece of arithmetic. Then she said, "You can call me by my proper name if you like."

"I'm glad. It's a beautiful name – Lila."

"I'm sick of my nickname. I pretended to myself I didn't mind being called Stench. But really I hate it. The trouble is, after you've been in this place long enough, you have to pretend to yourself that nothing matters. But it does, doesn't it?"

There was a long silence. Then Stench looked downhearted. "I suppose I'm never going to get the Device now."

"Why not?"

"You heard what the Controller said. They put the rubbish on the incinerator. I don't know how you got away with it before. But I know you won't want to go again. And even if you were brave enough – or mad enough – to go, you'd never come back."

"What nonsense! Of course I'm going," Little Fearless said, pretending that she couldn't care less.

Stench looked amazed. "You mustn't, Little Fearless. It's not worth it just to steal something."

At this Little Fearless paused, wondering if she could trust Stench. Somehow, as she looked at her worried face, she felt that she could.

"I'll make it into the City all right. And I'm not going to try and steal anything this time."

"You're not?"

"No. I'm going to find our families. That's why I've been trying to get out from the start. And I'll keep a special look-out for yours – Lila."

With this, Little Fearless jumped onto Stench's shoulders and pitched herself into the rubbish container from which Lady Luck and Bellyache and the Whistler had recently emerged. She heard Stench's voice hissing at her from outside.

"You'll be killed!"

"Don't you want to see your family again?"

There was a pause. Then, just before the rubbish container began to move, Little Fearless heard a whisper.

"More than anything in the world. Good luck, Little Fearless."

The Final Journey

Lock out the world and let yourself in.

Advertising slogan of
Omikron Gated Communities

What seemed like only a minute or so later, Little Fearless's container was outside, and its contents – Little Fearless included – emptied into the rubbish lorry. Then, as before, the vehicle started its journey away from the Institute.

Little Fearless inspected her surroundings in the dim light. The usual revolting muck and useless trash. Mouldy food, a ruined old hearthrug that stank of urine, a broken laundry mangle, bits and pieces of anonymous busted metal and wood. She climbed over the piles of garbage so she could look out of the back.

This time, the lorry did not stop at all. It chugged and whizzed right through the City. Little Fearless peered out into the darkness and watched the City begin to diminish behind her. She craned her neck round the side of the lorry so she could see where they were heading. There, blotting out the horizon, was a huge blaze.

Little Fearless searched desperately for a solution. She couldn't let her story end this way. She thought about throwing herself out, but the vehicle was moving too fast. She considered giving herself up to the man with the beard and the scar, but she didn't trust him, and didn't think she could make herself heard anyway.

The lorry drew closer and closer to the flames; Little Fearless could feel the heat. The vehicle reversed right up to the incinerator and stopped. A great orange glow filled her vision and scorched her face. There was the slam of a door as the driver got out. He activated the mechanism and the back of the lorry began to tilt. Bit by bit the rubbish began to tremble out onto the fire.

Little Fearless held on for dear life, and looked around frantically for something to save her. Her eyes alighted on the damp old hearthrug. It was rolled up and tied with string, but there was a small hole in the middle. As quick as she could, struggling to find her footing, she pushed herself into the middle of the carpet. Seconds later, she felt a bump and a jolt and she was out of the lorry and surrounded by intense heat. But the carpet was rolling, as she had hoped, and using the weight of her body she kept it rolling until it travelled past the fire and onto some muddy ground on the other side. It was scorching hot, but the dampness and thickness of the rug had saved her from burning alive. Wheezing and choking from the smoke, she fought her way out of the carpet.

Little Fearless hadn't seriously injured herself, but the shock of the close escape and the fall from the back of the lorry, even cushioned by the rug, seemed to have set all the bones in her body trembling. She was dazed and stunned, and, with the mud, rubbish and white ash from the fire all over her, looked more bizarre than ever. She took a few deep breaths and tried to compose herself.

She made her way to a main road, along which cars whizzed every few seconds. In front of her was a small single-decker bus picking up passengers; it seemed to be heading in the direction she wanted. With a leap, she was on the back bumper. She held on for fifteen minutes until the driver spotted her in the rear-view mirror and she was forced to let go and walk. It was a journey that seemed to take for ever – and as usual she had very little time. As she walked she tried to think, but no clear thoughts would come. It was as if the cold wind and the choking ash in her lungs had fogged the inside of her head.

Eventually she made her way to sector six, where Beauty's parents lived. She found it easy to navigate her way through the neighbourhood, which was lush and prosperous. There were wide avenues and spotless streets, and houses that were more like mansions, with great gravel paths and Gothic pillars. Security patrol cars cruised the streets at regular intervals, and more than once Little Fearless had to duck behind a tree in case she was spotted. The way she looked, there was little hope that she might be mistaken for one of the rich kids who lived in this area.

She was just about to turn the corner into Beauty's parents' street when she saw a puddle of flashing blue light on the ground and heard the sudden whine of a siren behind her.

She looked round and saw a security patrol car drawing to a halt. A man wearing the uniform of the City Protection Company – a division of the Omikron Gated Communities – emerged. He was tall and heavily built, with a face that was neither stern nor kindly but trained to look blank and neutral. Little Fearless's eyes darted around, looking for some means of escape, but she had no chance. She decided to stand her ground. Little Fearless racked her brains for some seed of an idea that would save her.

"Good evening," said the security guard. His voice was not unfriendly, and he seemed to be viewing Little Fearless's dishevelled and muck-covered appearance with amusement rather than suspicion. "And what might you be up to?"

The fog in her head suddenly cleared, leaving her mind sharp and pure. She gave a bright, breezy smile and said, with complete confidence and cheerfulness, "Well – what do you think?" She gave a little bow and turned round.

"I'm not sure," said the security guard neutrally. "What do I think about what?"

"My costume, of course, silly," she said. "My friend's having a fancy dress party. Her daddy is a director of one of the Ten Corporations, and it's going to be great fun. But instead of us all getting dressed up, she wants us to come looking poor. Isn't that hilarious? The theme is beggars, outcasts and narcoholics. It's this season's look. This took me about two hours to get right. Do you like it? Do I look really, really, horrible?"

"Where's the party?"

"It's just down here." She spoke the names of Beauty's parents, and the security guard looked impressed. "There's going to be a prize for the best costume – a week on a private island in the Sunlands – and I'm bound to win. My smells are just the best. I had to send my daddy's chauffeur all over the nastiest bits of the City to find the worst-smelling stuff. And these clothes I had made by a theatrical company, retailored from the clothes of genuine homeless people. They're so witty and clever, don't you agree?"

"I need to ask you a question," said the security man flatly.

Little Fearless braced herself. Now she was sure to be caught.

"Are you a boy or are you a girl?"

Little Fearless pretended to be shocked and offended. "How dare you! What do I look like, for heaven's sake?"

"Well," said the guard cautiously, not quite sure whether he was dealing with a deranged vagrant or the child of a rich and powerful family, "to be honest, you look vaguely like a boy."

"Of course I'm a boy," said Little Fearless indignantly, lowering her voice slightly to make it sound huskier and more masculine. "I know it's a good costume, but you've got eyes in your head, haven't you? You should get yourself some spectacles, or you'll always be going around arresting the wrong people."

The security guard paused. They had had a call saying that there might be a girl loose in the City who had run away from the City Community Faith School, but this apparition didn't look like any girl he'd ever seen. His shift was nearly over, and he didn't want to get into trouble for arresting someone whose wealthy family could probably get him sacked if the son – if it really was a boy – took enough offence.

"It's a fantastic outfit," he said, smiling. He turned back to his car. "You're bound to win. I've never seen such a sight in all my life."

"And what about my smell?" demanded Little Fearless. "What do you think of that? It took me hours to work out how to stink like a proper poor person."

The security guard laughed, and opened the car door. "You smell absolutely terrible," he told her, climbing into the car. "Have a nice holiday in the Sunlands."

He started the engine and drove off, waving to Little Fearless as he went. Little Fearless waved back, and then quickly covered the hundred yards to the home of Beauty's parents.

The house was immaculate. It was set in large grounds, with expanses of manicured lawns and tidy flower beds, and was illuminated by hidden spotlights in the front garden, which was the size of the whole exercise yard for the thousand girls at the Institute. The house was painted candy pink, and had huge stone columns at the front which supported the roof to a large porch. There were lights on behind high windows, and an immense triple garage off to the far side. The house was hemmed in by high railings three times the size of Little Fearless, and she knew she could not climb them. Besides, there were signs that said BEWARE OF THE DOGS, and she had heard distant barking from behind the house.

There were large double gates at the entrance, with a speaker grille and a series of buttons. Little Fearless decided she had no choice but to press the buzzer. She waited for somebody to answer, but instead an electronic voice issued from the loudspeaker. It was bright and affable, but entirely artificial.

"Good evening, and welcome to Sanctuary Mansion. If you have an appointment, please press *one*. If you know your security code, please press *two*. If you are a vendor or a street salesman, or a collector for charity, please move on swiftly. For any other enquiries, please press *three*."

Little Fearless could barely reach the buttons, and had to stretch up on tiptoe to press *three*. Another electronic voice manifested itself.

"Good evening. None of the housekeeping staff are available at present. Please leave a message after the tone and we will attend to you as soon as possible. Thank you for calling."

Little Fearless felt irritated. This was hopeless. Nevertheless, she began speaking into the grille, feeling vaguely foolish. "I have come from the Institute, I mean the City Community Faith School, so that I can—"

At that point the loudspeaker let out a long beep and announced, "Thank you for your message. Unfortunately the night staff are occupied with other duties at the moment, and will attend to you as soon as they have a chance. Thank you for waiting."

Little Fearless heard a car engine in the distance, and wondered if it was the security man on his rounds again. She pressed the buzzer again, and the voice repeated itself, asking her to leave a message. This time she tried to speak as quickly as she could.

"Your daughter is in trouble. I have a bottle of tears that—"

But again the machine interrupted. "Thank you for your message. The memory is now full and your message could not be saved. Your visit is much appreciated. Please wait until the night staff have an opportunity to attend to your needs."

The machine fell silent. Little Fearless pounded at the gates with her tiny fists. An answering cry of barks and growls came, and several huge dogs began to slouch around the tidy bushes and shrubs. Little Fearless sighed hopelessly, and looked desperately around her. Ten feet to her right was a letter box marked SANCTUARY MANSION.

She felt in her pocket for the letter that Beauty had given her. The flap was open, the glue melted by the heat of her body. In her haste, as she fumbled with it, the letter fell into a puddle. She picked it up and shook it off. She'd better check that was still readable, she thought. She didn't know what was in it, but she felt pretty certain what the tone would be. Beauty was proud and haughty, and furious with her parents. Little Fearless expected the note to give them a dressing-down in no uncertain terms and demand that they come and fetch her right away.

In the reflected light from the illuminated garden, she read Beauty's message written in slightly shaky pencil, blurred by water from the puddle.

> Dear Mum and Dad,
>
> I am so sory for everything I did. I'm sory I was not a creddit to you and that I made you a shaymed. Plese come and get me. I cant stand this place. I feel so ugly and alone. Plese come and save me. It is terible here.
>
> Plese lissen to Little Fereless, who is the bravest person I have ever nown. Everything she says is true.
>
> Love—

And there was Beauty's real name, which until then Little Fearless had never known.

The sound of the engine drew nearer. She could see a blue light flickering through the trees. She knew if the security guard saw her now, she would have no chance of pulling the wool over his eyes again. Hurriedly she put the letter back in the envelope, thrust it in the letter box and fled as fast as she could.

Little Fearless trudged towards Angel Square, her heart puckering into a dry pouch of disappointment. The small bottle of tears felt like a heavy rock in her pocket.

The houses were small and boring again now – all much the same, all quite pleasant. As on her previous two visits, ordinary houses full of ordinary people lined ordinary streets. She thought about knocking on a door. But what was the point? Even if they did believe her, one single ordinary family would not be able to do anything. There was no point if the police weren't interested, and the Church wasn't interested, and the City Boss and all the politicians were in cahoots with the Controller, and the rich people wouldn't let you anywhere near them, protected as they were by fences and dogs, and by servants and machines and security guards.

Then she saw something that gave her the feeling of what-must-be.

Through one of the windows of one of the most ordinary of the ordinary houses, she could see yet another ordinary family: a mother, a father, a daughter and a son, all staring at the vast vidscreen that covered an entire wall of their front room.

The remarkable thing was, Little Fearless recognized the father.

He had a small scrubby beard and a thin white scar. He was the rubbish-lorry driver – Little Fearless was certain of it, even though she had only ever glimpsed him in the darkness.

He had changed out of his work clothes; he must have just finished his shift. If she were Stargazer, she thought, she would be sure that this was a sign. So without hesitation, she marched up the path and rang the bell, which let out a deafening jangle. As it rang, the family's expressions remained unchanged. Nobody got up.

Hot-headed as ever, Little Fearless felt a shock of anger rush through her. She had not come all this way just to be ignored for some stupid vidscreen programme. She leaned on the doorbell so it kept on ringing.

After several minutes, the door finally opened. It was the man with the beard and the scar.

"Do you know what time it is?" he said sternly, looking disapprovingly at Little Fearless's filthy clothes.

"I don't have a watch," said Little Fearless sadly, thinking of her father's silver watch that she had given to Stench.

"It's one minute to ten. The big prize quiz has just finished, and the touchball game between the City and the Out of Cityers is about to begin."

There was a pause.

Little Fearless started to speak. "I've got something very important—"

"We are all very upset. We don't like people ringing on our doorbell at any time, but to ring when we are just home from work is positively bad manners, and to ring when we are watching the vidscreen is almost beyond—"

"SHUT UP!" bellowed Little Fearless.

The man looked as if someone had just slapped him. "How … how dare you speak to me like that," he said, his face darkening, his scar turning crimson. But he didn't shut the door.

"My name is Little Fearless, and I have escaped from the Institute."

"The Institute?" repeated the man blankly.

"The City Community Faith School, but it's not a school. I say 'escaped' because it is actually a children's prison. You don't know me, but I know you. You drive the rubbish lorry. It's an awful place, and the Controller keeps us all in rags, and we get sick, and some of the girls have died, and we are like slaves, and it is horrible. I can prove it too."

With this she reached into her pocket and drew out the perfume bottle filled with tears. "This bottle is filled with the tears of the children at the Institute. It is the proof of our misery."

She held out the bottle. The man looked down at her, clearly shocked. Because, like the policeman and the priest, he was not a bad person, and he loved his own children. But he didn't understand more than he wanted to about the world, because it made him uncomfortable and unhappy to think about such unsettling things, even if they were true. *Especially* if they were true.

"That can't be the case," said the man, not taking the bottle.

"Why?" said Little Fearless. "Because I'm only a child?"

"No, not at all," he responded. "I know it isn't true because if it was I would have seen it on the vidscreen."

"That," said Little Fearless, "is stupid. The vidscreen, from what I've seen of it, is like … it's like a … a pantomime on the edge of a battlefield. It distracts you from seeing what's important right there in front of your eyes."

"What do you mean?" he asked, looking puzzled.

Some light appeared in the man's eyes, some light of intelligence and recognition that momentarily gave Little Fearless a flicker of hope.

"I do think I know you from somewhere…" he said haltingly.

Then a voice rang out from the front room. "John! It's starting."

The man's eyes went blank again as he looked down at Little Fearless. "I'm really terribly sorry," said the man called John. "I have to go now. I really would like to help you, but the touchball game is about to begin."

"It's started, John," came the voice again.

A woman appeared by his side. She was tall, pale, thin-lipped, and plainly in a hurry. "Who's she?"

"She says her name is Little Frightful, or something. She says she's from the City Community Faith School."

"What's she doing here then, interrupting our vidscreen?" said the woman crossly.

"She says it's not a school at all but a prison."

"What nonsense!" The woman made a snorting sound like a horse.

"She says she can prove it."

"Garbage," said the woman. "I'm calling the school to complain. The cheek of it!" And with that she disappeared.

The man looked worried and somewhat guilty. "I'm most terribly sorry," he said. "I really have to go. Thank you so much for stopping by. If I see something about it on the vidscreen, I'll certainly think about getting in touch with the authorities."

Little Fearless gave a sad smile of resignation. She tried one last time to thrust the bottle of tears into his hands. The man hesitated, then shook his head and slowly turned away. He shut the door in her face.

Little Fearless stood there for what seemed like a very long time staring at the closed door.

Then she turned and threw the bottle of tears into a rubbish bin beside the front gate. With her heart in her boots, she made her way to Angel Square for what she knew would be the last time.

When she reached the square a few minutes later, she sat down by the fountain where the angels stood, their lips dry of water, their once beautiful faces worn and decayed. She stared at the angels and spoke to them softly. "Truth, Courage and Compassion. How corny! What a joke!"

It seemed to her that their blank faces stared back at her, as if trying to communicate some mute, ancient message. In her tiredness and despair, she carried on muttering to them.

"You don't know anything – you're so crumbled down and broken. Where are the fountains that once sprang from your mouths? You're dumb. You don't know the answers to any of my questions."

Little Fearless was talking loudly now.

"Why won't the people see when they have a million eyes? And what about Eidolon? *Is* there just one god? Are there a hundred gods? Is there no god at all? Are we at the Institute nothing, just because we have no one?"

Little Fearless picked up a pebble and threw it wildly at the nearest angel. It bounced off a wing and fell into the dry base of the fountain.

"There are so many whys, and I'm just a poor, stupid girl who's hot-headed, stubborn and untidy. My head hurts from not understanding. My heart hurts from being alone."

Now she stood, a lonely figure in the square, and screamed at the night sky, "Where are your answers?"

The statues were silent. All she could hear was the wind, which blew just as coldly and as relentlessly as before. Her heart sank still further into her boots. She looked back at the angels and muttered to herself, "Stupid angels. Stupid people. Stupid me for telling stupid stories."

Little Fearless turned away from where the angels stood mutely on their crumbling plinth and inspected the square. This time the holiday coach was not there. Just an empty space.

She did not care. She no longer believed that there was a place called the Sunlands. Or if there was, it would rain and be cold all the time. Names, she had learned, meant nothing. The Institute called itself a school but was a prison. The people in the City were people the same as she was, had children just like her, but they behaved as if she were an animal because of her appearance and her bad luck to have ended up where she had. Eidolon was meant to look after everyone, but it seemed he only helped people who were neat and tidy and had giant vidscreens and expensive cars.

She had to go back to the Institute. She knew that if she just disappeared, the other girls would pay the price. She had to go back, admit her failure and take the blame. She assumed the man's wife had been as good as her word and had telephoned the Controller.

So it was that less than an hour later, still not afraid, but sad and rather lonely, Little Fearless found herself back in Hall Seven.

Oroborous Unmasked

You have no name.
You have no family.
You have no past.
Only when you understand this
will you have a future.

The Controller

The lights were still out, and everything seemed to be quiet. Little Fearless allowed herself a bit of hope. Perhaps the woman had been so absorbed by the vidscreen that she'd forgotten to phone the Institute.

When she approached her bunk, she sensed that something was wrong but couldn't work out what. As she began to undress, she saw that her pillows seemed different somehow, but she was too tired to care.

She crouched down to see if Stargazer was awake. There was just a shape under the blankets. Little Fearless decided that the bad news could wait. She tenderly touched the shape, and blew Stargazer a silent kiss. Wearily she removed the last of her clothes. She couldn't even be bothered to put on her pyjamas. She took a look around the dormitory. She could hear the slow breathing of the girls from the beds all around her. She felt overcome by exhaustion.

She pulled back the sheets, yawning. Then her face froze in a mask of horror.

Lying there, fully dressed in her uniform, was Lady Luck, her marble eyes wide open and her face set in a terrible, triumphant smile.

"Surprise," she said, in her fake-sweet voice.

Little Fearless reeled back. She heard another voice – a man's.

"You're late."

She spun round. The Controller had emerged like a phantom out of the shadows. Behind him, the Whistler had her arm round Stargazer's neck. She pulled back the covers of Stargazer's bed to reveal a scattering of pillows. Stench and Bellyache stood behind the Whistler. Stench looked like she was about to speak, but Little Fearless gave a little shake of her head. Lady Luck silently rose from the bed and seized Little Fearless fiercely by the shoulders. She did not struggle.

"So the woman phoned you after all," said Little Fearless flatly, almost to herself.

"Woman. What woman?" said the Controller almost cheerfully. "No one has telephoned."

"Oh," said Little Fearless. She looked around, and saw that Tattle was awake in the neighbouring bunk staring at her. "Tattle. I forgive you," she said softly. "I know you didn't mean it."

But Tattle shook her head violently. "I didn't tell anyone, Little Fearless," she said. "I swear."

"It's all right, Tattle. You can't help who you are. I should never have told you about the plan in the first place. It was my fault."

"Actually, she's telling the truth," said the Controller.

"But … but I don't understand," said Little Fearless, bewildered. "How did you find out?"

Now the Controller looked at Stargazer, who was still in the Whistler's grip. She was holding herself absolutely rigid.

"*She* betrayed you," he said matter-of-factly, nodding at Stargazer. "Your very best friend of all."

Little Fearless turned her gaze on Stargazer, whose face now looked anguished and contorted.

"What is he talking about, Stargazer?"

At first Stargazer didn't answer, but simply stared at the floor. But finally, after a long silence, she did speak, her voice cracked and marbled with guilt.

"It's true."

Little Fearless couldn't believe what she was hearing. The world seemed to swim before her eyes. Stargazer was welling up with tears. She spoke again, more urgently this time, as if pleading for forgiveness.

"I told on you. It was never Tattle, always me. I told them about the stories you told us. That's how the Controller knew about them. If I didn't spy for them, they threatened to have you taken away.

"Then you made your plans to escape. After that I decided to keep quiet, and tried to throw the Controller off the scent by making stuff up about it being other girls, not you at all. But in the end, I believed my vision was going to come true. That you were going to die if you kept trying to escape. So I told on you. But not until this final time, when I felt you were in the most danger. That's why the X girls were waiting for you at the rubbish bins. I tried to talk you out of going, and I thought I could. But you wouldn't change your mind."

Little Fearless was silent.

"Say something, Little Fearless. Don't you see – I did it for you. I had to stop you dying. I had to. I betrayed you because I love you, Little Fearless."

Stargazer burst into tears. Little Fearless smiled sadly.

"You see, Z73. No one can be trusted. That is why we need rules. They are the only things you can rely on, in the end," said the Controller quietly.

Now Bellyache seized Little Fearless as well. She and Lady Luck stood either side of her, their fingers gripping her hard enough to raise vivid red marks on her skin. She was still undressed and she seized her old tweed jacket to try to cover herself up.

The Controller made an announcement in a voice loud enough to wake the slumbering girls. "Everyone awake and out of their beds. Right now."

And within a few minutes, everyone was up, standing and gaping at the forlorn figure of Little Fearless, naked apart from a ragged jacket. Stargazer was still crying. Stench looked unhappy and puzzled. But the Whistler and Bellyache and

Lady Luck seemed to be thoroughly enjoying themselves. The girls stared at the sight in front of them. There was silence. No one moved a muscle. No one, not even Beauty, Soapdish or Tattle, spoke a word of protest.

"We have caught the child who left the protection of the school," said the Controller, his voice low and hypnotic. "Look at her carefully. Look at her, naked and pathetic and more lost than ever before. Take your *last* look. Then forget. Forget everything. It will be better for you all. Only in forgetting is there peace."

There was silence and stillness. Then the X girls started to take Little Fearless away. Still nobody moved and nobody said anything. Only Stargazer screamed and shouted.

"Stop them! It's Little Fearless, the bravest of the brave! If we lose her, we are all lost. If we forget her, we will all be forgotten. Stand and fight. There are more of us than them. Stand together!"

But it was just Stargazer, and no one took any notice of her.

Stargazer alone tried to push away the X girls as they led Little Fearless from the dormitory. Then she threw her arms around Little Fearless's neck and held on tight. Just before Lady Luck and the Whistler finally prised her away, Stargazer heard Little Fearless whisper something in her ear, something only she could hear.

Only then did she let go.

*   *   *

A few minutes later, Little Fearless found herself in a small darkened room in the Control Block facing the Controller. They were alone. Little Fearless shivered in her jacket. The Controller reached under the table and brought out a large plain woollen blanket. He handed it to Little Fearless. Eagerly she wrapped it around herself. She gazed at the Controller, waiting for what would happen next.

The Controller himself seemed unsure. After maybe a complete minute of silence had passed, his face resolved itself into a kind of tired resignation. He brought out a large, leather-bound book and let it drop onto the table in front of him with a dull thud.

"Do you know what this is, Little Fearless?" asked the Controller quietly. His voice sounded different to her. Less harsh, less dry, almost human. And he said her name – not her number, her *name* – without contempt.

Little Fearless shook her head and gathered the blanket tighter around her.

"It is the book of rules," he said simply.

"I know them already," she muttered, not prepared for another lecture about all the things she wasn't allowed to do in the Institute.

"You don't understand," he continued. "They are not *your* rules. They are *my* rules. They are issued to me by the City Boss and the Ten Corporations. Just as you have to follow rules, I also have to do what I am told."

There was another pause. The Controller seemed to be

struggling with himself. He looked down at the floor. When he looked up again, he almost seemed to be pleading with Little Fearless.

"I have devoted much of my life to following rules. After many difficult and painful experiences, I have learned that it is for the best, however hard and unfair it may seem. That is what I have tried to teach you in this place, Little Fearless. You are too young to make sense of the world. There are things I know that…" He paused, and seemed to gather himself for a second.

"There are things you don't know, and can't know. But believe me. *Believe me*. What is about to happen must happen. It must happen because it is in the rules. And without the rules, there is nothing. We are all lost."

Little Fearless gazed at him, her eyes wide. "What difficult and painful experiences?" she asked.

"I beg your pardon?" The Controller looked confused.

"You said you have had many difficult and painful experiences. What were they?"

Little Fearless held him in her gaze. Suddenly it was as if he were the captive, and she the one imprisoning *him*. He wriggled and shifted uncomfortably.

"You like stories, don't you?"

Little Fearless nodded.

"You think they make things easier. You think we are all the better off for telling stories to one another and to ourselves."

Little Fearless nodded again. The Controller grimaced as

if in pain, and then spoke again. "Let me tell *you* a story, then."

"Is it a true one?" she asked immediately.

The Controller didn't answer her question. He simply started speaking. At first his voice was so soft, Little Fearless could hardly hear him. But as he went on, his voice became stronger, louder, more powerful, almost as if it were a different person telling the story.

"Once there was a man. Just an ordinary man. A young man. He was young at a time when the City was still free. Before the bombs and the terror, and the law of the army and the police, and the City Boss, and before rule after rule after rule.

"He loved his freedom. He breathed it in. It enriched his blood; it made him ... so alive. He travelled, and read books, and had many friends. In those days, there were no identicards, no laws dictating what you could or couldn't say, or what kinds of jokes were allowed and what kinds forbidden. He met women. Many women. They liked him, but he liked his freedom too much to get involved with any of them. He kept his distance. He was a wanderer, and a rogue. Everyone smiled when he came their way. He was popular. Everyone wanted to be his friend.

"Then, without any warning, he fell in love."

The Controller faltered. It seemed he couldn't speak.

"Who did he fall in love with?" prompted Little Fearless softly.

"He fell in love with the most beautiful woman you could ever imagine. Not just beautiful in her face, but in her mind, you see. She was like … like a bubbling spring of water. She was like the south wind. She was like a wave of light curving into the blue depths of the ocean."

Little Fearless was amazed. The Controller's face had changed utterly. Always so dead and colourless, it actually seemed alive for the first time. He nodded to himself, smiling, as if remembering. Then his face settled into stone again, and his voice became once more dead and emotionless.

"Then the bombs came," he said, bitterness lacing his voice. "The worshippers of Ormazd decided they wanted to destroy the City Boss and the Ten Corporations. They hated the false god, Eidolon; they hated the Democrenes; they hated it all and they waged war against us."

The Controller fidgeted with his hair. Even through his tinted glasses it seemed that he could not meet Little Fearless's gaze, instead focusing on a spot just above her head.

"The City Boss and the Ten Corporations responded by taking away the freedoms that young man loved so much. The freedom to say what he wanted, to be who he wanted. The freedoms to read and watch what he wanted. The freedom to walk down the street unchallenged, without having to show papers to the police. All these things began to disappear. And the City Boss and the Ten Corporations became more and more powerful and tyrannical as the fear in the City grew and grew.

"When that happened, he started to hate the City Boss and the Ten Corporations. In fact, he even had sympathy for the lovers of Ormazd, because they were poor and dis-possessed and angry. He came to believe that his enemies' enemies had to be his friends. He couldn't blame *them* for what was happening to his beloved City. So he turned his anger instead on the City Boss and the Ten Corporations."

Now at last he seemed to look directly at Little Fearless. She could see herself reflected in his glasses. She saw her own face, pale but unafraid.

"He decided he had to do something about it. He became a freedom fighter. They called him a spartakan and a fomenter, but he was none of these things. He was fighting for liberty. In their eyes, though, he was simply an insurgent. He attacked the City government. He arranged protests. He even – Eidolon, help me – he even hurt people ... innocent people ... so that the City Boss would be under pressure to give the Cityzens back their freedom."

Now the Controller stopped, as if incapable of speaking any more. A cold, clammy atmosphere filled the room. Little Fearless could hear the distant sounds of voices and move-ments outside the four walls.

"They worked together – he and ... and the woman. The woman he loved. They were bold and brilliant. No one could capture them. Their plans were impeccable. They were outlaws and, to tell you the truth, they loved it. They believed that *their* god – not Eidolon, not Ormazd, but the god of human freedom – was on their side.

"The woman was amazing, Little Fearless. Amazing. She could run fast; she could talk fast; she could think fast. She was honest, and true, and like ... like ... like no one anybody had known before. He became famous, although it was she who was the brilliant one. He even had a nickname: Oroborous, the snake eating its tail. He was said to be the mastermind. The villain behind all the plots that ever were. But some of the people – the people who believed in freedom instead of tyranny – loved him.

"And then ... and then..." The Controller's voice faltered again, then strengthened into a monotone. "And then the light grew dark. The spring dried up. The wind was stilled."

"What...?" asked Little Fearless.

"The woman died," said the Controller, chewing on his fingernails.

It seemed he was going to end the story there. He picked up the leather-bound book and stood up. But as soon as Little Fearless said, "How did she die?" he sat meekly back down again, and continued.

"She was blown up by an Outlander's bomb. By a fanatical worshipper of Ormazd. She had said something that they believed insulted their god. So they killed her like a dog. Blew up the car she and three others were in. All of them died. And someone else died too. The young man died, although he was nowhere near the car. Although he hadn't even a scratch on him."

Little Fearless nodded. She felt like a priest taking confession. She looked directly at the Controller. He was shaking. Then she spoke.

"And who was he? Who was this man?" she asked gently.

The Controller didn't answer. Instead he very slowly rolled up the right sleeve of his shirt, exposing his arm. Just above the wrist, he picked at the flesh. Then, horribly, the skin began to peel back.

It took Little Fearless a couple of seconds to realize that the skin wasn't skin at all, but a thin, flesh-coloured plastic strip designed to blend in exactly with the rest of his arm.

Underneath the plastic was the tattoo of a snake eating its own tail.

"Oroborous!" gasped Little Fearless.

The Controller shook his head and slowly pulled the strip of plastic back over the tattoo.

"Oroborous is dead," he said flatly. "He died when the woman he loved died. After that he realized that freedom was a trick and a ruse, and a lie. That there was nothing – nothing – more important than law and order. That the madness of the fanatics must be crushed at all costs. So he surrendered himself to the City Boss, and said he would do everything he could in his power to help him bring the insurgency under control."

He laughed suddenly, a bitter, knowing laugh that was ugly to hear.

"They were clever, I'll give them that. Anybody less intelligent would have announced the capture of Oroborous and paraded him before the crowds. But no. They understood – they still do – that the people need a bogeyman to keep them in order and afraid. So even now they pretend that Oroborous continues to roam free, blowing up people and buildings, the police always getting closer and closer, but never quite catching him. As long as Oroborous is at large, the City is in grave danger, and they can do anything – anything at all – to try and ensure his capture. But of course, the moment they actually catch him, the period of fear will be over, and they will have to start relaxing all the rules again. And they love the rules – because they love power. Like all governments.

"It was after they captured me that they decided to set up the school. The *Institute*. It struck them as amusing to make me its controller. Me. The man who tried to bring the City freedom, now responsible for imprisoning children – *children* – without trial or hope of release. They realized it would simultaneously punish me and make me useful. And I turned out to be a good administrator, an excellent Controller. Why? Because I no longer believe in freedom. Because I believe in order at any cost. At – any – cost."

As he spat out these last words, the Controller regarded the book of rules again. Then he looked up at Little Fearless.

Sighing, his voice reverted again into one of sadness and resignation.

"That is all there is. The rules. Nothing beyond the rules. And the rules tell me quite clearly what is to be done with any child who tries to escape from the Institute. I am here to carry those rules out. And they *shall* be carried out."

At this a change suddenly came over the Controller. It was as if his normal self had suddenly appeared again, even deader and colder than before.

"You need to learn, girl. You need to learn the truth about the world, just as I did."

He rose and made to leave.

"But why?" asked Little Fearless urgently. "Why are you telling me this?"

The Controller shook his head almost violently. "No, no, no, no, no." He began to walk towards the door. "You think I am cruel. But I am not. Not *that* cruel, no. I just carry out what needs to be done. What the City Boss and the Ten Corporations tell me needs to be done and said. You don't need to know any more. What I have told you is explanation enough."

"But—"

The Controller held up his hand. "You are right to hate me, Z73. Hate me all you need. For there are worse things than hate. Truly there are. I know that far better than you can imagine."

"But," said Little Fearless, desperate for more information, "why Oroborous? Why the snake that ate its own tail?"

"Because that," said the Controller slowly and with infinite sadness, "is what people do."

In the days and nights that followed, there was much talk about Little Fearless.

Many of the children were adamant that she had got what she deserved. Soapdish, Beauty and Tattle, while upset at losing their friend, became angry at Little Fearless because it was less painful than feeling sorry for her. Stargazer stood up for Little Fearless and said that she was a hero and that everyone should try to be like her. But nobody listened to her.

A few other children, Z girls, the lowest of the low, stood by Stargazer, and talked, and told stories at night of the legend of Little Fearless. Occasionally graffiti would appear scrawled on the walls: *Never forget Little Fearless* or the letters *LF*.

The Controller was clever, though. Now that Little Fearless was gone, most of the girls noticed that although the Institute was still terrible, it was very slightly less terrible since Little Fearless had disappeared.

Then he promoted Little Fearless's friends – Tattle, Beauty and Soapdish – to X girls, where they learned to bully and be lofty and arrogant. Tattle, when she did imitations of people nowadays, no longer copied X girls or the Controller, but instead ridiculed Y and Z children. Beauty loved her new uniform, and as they had proper mirrors in the Control

Block, where the X girls lived, she spent a lot of time attending to her face and hair, which she was allowed to grow again. And Soapdish was delighted to be where there was plenty of soap, and where everything was tidy and in proper order.

The Controller never referred to Little Fearless again when addressing the children at the Sunday Gatherings, and he instructed all the X girls to do the same. Some of the Y and Z girls still talked about her and some told stories. But, after a while, the talking and the stories faded. After a little more time had passed, the X girls began to hint that there had never been any such person as Little Fearless.

That she herself was just a story.

At first, the children thought this was mad – to think that anyone could believe that something that had really happened was just a story. But then, when they thought about it, no one could remember very clearly what Little Fearless had looked like. All the Y and Z girls had, for a long time, looked the same and dressed the same. And Little Fearless had, in those last days, been hard to distinguish from all the other girls. They had no history books to remind them of what had happened in the past, and no newspapers to tell them what was happening in the present. So more and more of the children began to wonder if the things Little Fearless had done were just in their imaginations.

The Controller instructed his spies to repeat, with absolute certainty, that there had never been any such person. The other girls, faced with such unshakeable convictions, began to lose faith in their own memories. Eventually, any time anybody did mention her, someone was bound to say "Don't waste your time on make-believe" or "If you believe in that, you'll believe in anything" or even "Good words make history; bad words make misery."

However, there was one person left who was absolutely sure that there had been someone called Little Fearless.

The last thing Little Fearless had whispered to Stargazer was "Remember me." And Stargazer had sworn to herself that she would remember, come what may. To anyone who would listen, she would say, "But you *must* remember Little Fearless. She was the bravest and the best."

However, the other girls didn't want to listen. Their guilt and their shame at abandoning Little Fearless was too great. After a while, they began to say that Stargazer was mad. After all, that was why she had been brought to the Institute in the first place. Eventually a day came when even Stargazer herself began to think she was mad, just as the doctors at the orphanage had once told her.

Perhaps, thought Stargazer, Little Fearless is just one of my strange visions. Someone who never existed after all.

One day, the Controller sent his three chief X girls into the Work Block to find out who still believed in Little Fearless.

Lady Luck saw Stargazer working quietly in the laundry, scrubbing away stains and spots from the clothes. She spoke loudly, in front of all the other girls. "Look, there's that mind-crip who thinks there really was such a person as Little Fearless."

And slowly, deliberately, Stargazer turned her head and snapped, before anyone could laugh at her, "No, it's a lie."

Bellyache cast a stony glance at Stargazer. "It's true. She believes that there was once a girl who went to the City in the back of a rubbish lorry."

Some of the other girls started sniggering and pointing at Stargazer.

"There never *was* such a person," insisted Stargazer.

The Whistler stared at her doubtfully. Stargazer turned on her angrily. "There was no one. No girl has ever escaped from the Institute. No one ever will." Then she turned back to her laundry and began scrubbing twice as hard as before.

So, that day, Lady Luck, Bellyache and the Whistler reported back to the Controller that there were no girls left in the Institute who believed Little Fearless had ever existed. The Controller looked satisfied behind his tinted spectacles, and decided that the matter was now well and truly closed.

The Pit

Do not enter. Danger of death.

Temporary sign outside
the Discipline Block

Just as the children in the Institute had ceased to believe in Little Fearless, some people in the City were beginning to acknowledge her existence.

The reason the woman from the house that Little Fearless had visited had never phoned the Institute was because her husband, John, had asked her not to. In fact, that same night, John the rubbish collector had done something remarkable. Thinking of Little Fearless's tired, desperate face, he had risen from his chair in the middle of the touchball game.

Then he had switched off the vidscreen.

His family had screamed and shouted and made him turn it on again. But like the policeman and the priest, he had a thought in his head that he couldn't make go away.

The morning after Little Fearless had visited, while he was putting out the rubbish, his eyes were momentarily blinded by a glitter of reflected sunlight. He blinked, dazzled. When he opened his eyes again, he saw that the glare was coming from a small glass bottle in the dustbin. For a long moment he stared at it. Then he gently picked it up, careful not to drop it, and took it inside.

That day, he happened to be working in the university zone. He was acquainted with a scientist who lived there, and John handed him the bottle and asked him to find out what exactly was in it. Later the same week, when John was collecting his rubbish again, the scientist handed the bottle back and told him that extensive and conclusive analysis in his laboratory had revealed that the bottle was full of children's tears. Twelve thousand, seven hundred and three to be precise.

That's an awful lot of unhappiness, by anyone's reckoning, thought John.

He stared at the bottle of tears night after night. He started to have odd thoughts. So odd, in fact, that he showed the bottle of tears to his neighbours. Who also started to have odd thoughts.

The story of the bottle of tears began to spread like a virus around the City. People began writing to newspapers and phoning radio stations to see if it could be true. The rumour that the Institute was really a prison full of miserable girls, and not the City Community Faith School for Retraining, Opportunity and Hope, persisted and grew.

Finally the Cityzens started to boycott the laundry at the Institute. Profits began to plummet. That was the final straw. Something had to be done.

The City Boss announced that although he could not open the Institute to the public – issues of national security prevented it – he would take round a small group of hand-picked reporters and cameramen in order to prove that the City Community Faith School was exactly what he said it was.

But many of the Cityzens were still not happy with this. So they decided to organize a Bottle of Tears demonstration outside the Institute for the same day as the City Boss's visit.

The first thing the City Boss did when he was faced with the prospect of opening the Institute to the vidcams was to phone the Controller and tell him to prepare for the visit.

Thus, over the next few weeks, the Institute underwent a complete transformation. The barbed wire that lined the top of the fifty foot high walls was removed and put into storage, ready to be erected again after the vidcams had left. The black metal walls were painted pale pink and covered with fake ivy to make them match the attractive walls outside the Institute.

The Discipline Block was disguised to look like an electricity substation. Notices were put up that read: *Do not enter. Danger of death.* The Food Block was temporarily turned into a refreshment zone, serving tasty snacks and hot drinks. The Y and Z girls kept their dreary grey clothes, but they were all made to clean and iron them immaculately so they looked smart and well turned out. The X girls' relaxation area and the Controller's garden were temporarily opened to the other girls. The small study area in the Work Block was extended and filled with books from charity shops.

All in all, the place began to look more like a school than a prison. But things inside were just as bad as ever. All the girls were threatened with dire punishments if they said anything uncomplimentary or unflattering to the reporters.

The only girl who might have had the courage to speak out had been entirely forgotten.

A week before the City Boss's visit, Stargazer happened to be wandering past the rubbish tips. As she walked by she heard the sound of sobbing. She looked just to the left of a pile of worn-out boots, and just to the right of a tower of rotting potatoes.

There, sitting on the ground, was Stench.

Stargazer wasn't quite sure what to do. Seeing Stench there made her feel uncomfortable. First and foremost, it brought back memories of Little Fearless, which Stargazer found confusing since she had recently decided that there was no such person. Secondly, she was bewildered to see an X girl crying.

Cautiously Stargazer approached the big, round-headed, red-faced X girl. And as she drew closer, she saw that Stench was clutching three things that she immediately recognized.

A bronze photo frame, a man's silver wristwatch, and a golden locket.

As soon as she saw these, Stargazer knew right away once more that Little Fearless was not just a story but a real flesh and blood person, and a hero, and her best friend. Suddenly filled with remorse for forgetting about her, she sat on the ground next to Stench and began to cry with her.

"Who are you?" asked Stench, still clutching the locket, the frame and the watch.

"Little Fearless was my best friend," said Stargazer.

At the mention of Little Fearless's name, Stench sobbed even harder. "Me too," said Stench. "In fact, she was my only friend."

Stench shook her head and took a deep breath. "She was the bravest girl I ever knew," she said. "She gave me these beautiful things. I think they belonged to my family, you know."

Stargazer felt surprised, but made sure she showed nothing on her face. If Stench had come to believe that these were memories of her own family, and if it helped her to get through the days, she didn't want to say anything to make her doubt it.

"This is a frame with a photograph of my grandparents. This is a watch which once belonged to my father. And this is a golden locket with a picture of my mother on her wedding day. I wanted to sell them to buy the Device. But then, after I'd looked at them long enough, I decided I didn't want the Device any more. What I wanted was my family. And there was only one girl who could help me find them.

"She had so much courage. The last time she went to the City, she thought she was going to be thrown on a bonfire, yet still she went. After she was caught and taken away, they bullied her and tormented her and called her names, but she never ever told any of the other X girls that I…" Stench looked at Stargazer cautiously, wondering if she could trust her.

Stargazer nodded reassuringly. "It's all right. Little Fearless told me all about how you helped her to escape. She said you helped her, even though you were an X girl. She said you were her friend. She said you were good – Lila."

Stench – Lila – looked distraught at this. "How I wish I could see her again and say sorry."

"Yes," said Stargazer. "I'm sorry too. Because I betrayed her – first by telling the Controller's spies that someone was going to try and escape, and then by forgetting her. And now she's disappeared and no one even believes that she was real."

"If only we could get her out of the Pit," moaned Stench.

At this, Stargazer suddenly stopped crying. "What?" she said.

"The Pit," repeated Stench blankly, as if it was obvious.

"What on earth is that?"

"Its real name isn't the Pit. Properly speaking, it's the CST – the Compound Sub Terra. But all the X girls call it the Pit. It's under the Discipline Block."

Stargazer blinked in amazement. "You mean she's still *here*? In the Institute?"

Stench stopped crying too and looked at Stargazer. "Of course." She lowered her voice and glanced towards the Discipline Block. "The Pit is where they put the ones that won't behave and won't ever believe what the Controller tells them. It goes very deep. There's a secret entrance. And down on the deepest level, there's a deeper cellar. It is cold and dark. You can only reach it by a long spiral staircase. That's the Pit. That's where they put the things and people that terrify and threaten them most. That is where Little Fearless has been ever since she was taken away."

"But I thought – I thought she was..."

"Dead? I'm surprised she's not," said Stench matter-of-factly. "I think the Controller must have a bit of a soft spot for her, because I've heard she gets more food and drink than people in the Pit usually get, and even a filthy blanket. Usually they've faded away within a few weeks, but Little Fearless is made of tough stuff. She's weak – very weak – but she's still there, so far as I know."

"Have you been there – inside the Pit?" asked Stargazer, excited now.

"No," said Stench. "Only the most senior X girls are allowed down there – Lady Luck, the Whistler and Bellyache. I only know about it because Bellyache likes to complain, and was moaning to herself about how cold it is down there when she thought no one was listening."

"But, Stench – we must go down there. We must rescue her."

"Rescue her?" said Stench, wiping her streaming nose with the sleeve of her uniform. "But how?"

"I don't know," replied Stargazer. She furrowed her brow and tried to concentrate. To help herself think, she started throwing pebbles from the ground at the mountain of worn-out boots. After she had thrown the sixth or seventh, the pile wobbled. She threw another. It wobbled again. Then with one last tiny pebble, so small you could barely see it, the whole huge pile collapsed in a great flurry.

Tiny pebbles one by one had brought down the whole lot.

And at that exact moment, Stargazer had her answer.

"Next week, the City Boss is coming to visit the Institute. He's going to inspect us all, in the exercise yard, the X girls too. So the Discipline Block will be unguarded. If we can slip away while he is here, we can rescue Little Fearless and show her to the City Boss. When he sees that girls are being starved, tormented and kept in *dungeons*, surely he'll have to do something."

Stench tried to think. And she didn't think very long before she said, "How am I going to get the keys?"

Stench had, attached to her belt, a ring with dozens of keys on it. Stargazer pointed to it. "Won't one of those open the door to the Pit?"

Stench shook her head. "No, these just open boring stuff like broom cupboards and laundry rooms. Only Lady Luck has all the important keys."

"Couldn't you swap them for a few hours, without her

noticing? After all, one set of keys looks pretty much like another."

"Suppose we could pull it off. What would it do? They'd only put her back inside again. The City Boss is probably in cahoots with the Controller."

Stargazer nodded. "But at least I'd see my best friend one last time and have a chance to say sorry."

"Yes," said Stench. "I would do anything to see Little Fearless again."

One week later, on the day when the City Boss was visiting the Institute, Stench and Stargazer were in the infirmary. Both had pretended to be too ill to attend, and had each drunk a pint of salt water to make themselves sick so that it would look convincing. It had worked – the last thing the Controller wanted was one of his girls throwing up all over the City Boss.

As good as her word, Stench had switched her set of keys with Lady Luck's that very morning while X1 was taking a shower. By now, all the children had worked hard to make the Institute look a lot more respectable and comfortable than it actually was, so that the City Boss and the Controller would be vindicated from the accusations that had been hurled at them from all seven sectors of the City.

Stargazer and Stench tiptoed out of the tiny infirmary and crept towards the Discipline Block, hoping that in all the fuss no one would notice they were missing.

The exercise yard was already filled with the rest of the girls, arranged into neat lines and wearing – for once – clean and well-pressed clothes. The City Boss was chatting affably with the Controller as they made their way up and down the rows of orderly, well-behaved and apparently contented children, and the vidcams filmed them, presenting a carefully constructed picture of serenity, order and good management.

Stargazer and Stench were just making their way past the now empty rubbish tips when Stargazer saw something that made her heartbeat accelerate.

Springing from the barren ground there was a blooming white rose.

It had grown exactly where the single tear had fallen from Little Fearless's blue eye when she gave her locket to Stench before escaping from the Institute for the final time. It was beautiful and perfect. Stargazer stared in awe at the gorgeous layers of lush ivory-coloured petals. Even Stench could not take her eyes off it.

Stargazer picked it and hid it inside her jacket to take as a gift for her best friend.

Down at the bottom of a steep spiral staircase underneath the Discipline Block, there crouched a small bedraggled girl, with one blue eye and one brown eye, who had long ago given up hope of anyone coming to rescue her.

She had been alone now in that hole for so long, she had forgotten almost entirely who she was and why she was there. The only people she saw down there were Lady Luck, the Whistler and Bellyache, who gave her just enough food to keep her alive and constantly reminded her that she wasn't even a number any more – not even a zero. She was a minus.

But still a sliver of her believed that she was not less than a zero, but that she was truly a real girl. Every day she fought to hold on to this belief; every day she tried to remember her name, and when she couldn't remember that, she even fought to remember the number she had been given.

On one occasion, the Controller briefly came to see her. He offered to let her out of the Pit. But there was one condition. She had to promise, from then on, to obey all the rules at all times, and try to make sure all the other girls did the same. Little Fearless refused. The Controller sighed a deep sigh and left her alone, promising to return if she changed her mind.

But she wouldn't change her mind. Not at any price.

She tried to keep her spirits up by telling herself that even if she herself was fading and getting weaker every day, then somehow she would live on in all the girls that she left behind. They would remember her, and she would give them hope. This gave her just enough strength to carry on breathing.

High above her, Stargazer and Stench had let themselves into the Discipline Block. As they had hoped, it was deserted. A dozen or so bleak cells with dirt floors lined either side of a corridor. Each had a filthy sink and a cracked and blocked-up toilet, and a small, hard bed.

"Where's the entrance to the Pit?" whispered Stargazer.

Stench indicated a blank wall at the end of the corridor, covered with peeling paint. "It's behind there."

"There's nothing there," wailed Stargazer despairingly. "It's just a wall."

"There's a secret mechanism that moves it," said Stench.

"Where?" asked Stargazer urgently.

There was a pause before Stench replied, "I'm not quite sure."

Stargazer raised her eyes to the heavens. While she had come to trust Stench completely, she had forgotten how dim-witted she was. If you didn't ask her a question directly, it was unlikely to occur to Stench herself.

"I should have thought about that, I suppose," said Stench slowly.

"Yes," said Stargazer, trying hard to keep the irritation and panic out of her voice. "Yes, you *should* have thought about that. Now, what are we going to do?"

Stench looked even blanker than she usually did. Stargazer gave a great sigh. She stared and stared at the wall as hard as she could, looking for some kind of clue.

After a few minutes had passed, she noticed a patch of wall that was discoloured in a slightly different way to the rest. It was hard to see, what with all the peeling paint and damp stains. But Stargazer had remarkably sensitive eyes, trained to notice the smallest of details after nights and nights of looking at the stars and trying to work out their meaning. She put her fingers on the mark and pressed. The wall itself seemed to move backwards slightly, and then what turned out to be a concealed door sprang open to reveal another door, this time with a clearly visible handle. Stargazer tried it. It was locked.

Stench stepped forward and began fumbling with the circle of keys that she had taken from Lady Luck. One of them fitted, and the door opened. Beyond it, dimly lit by flickering, naked bulbs, was a great spiral staircase.

They followed it down and down, very deep indeed. It got darker and darker and colder and colder. Eventually they reached a landing with an unmarked door.

"Could this be it?" asked Stargazer.

Stench pushed the door open.

Inside was a large room, starkly lit and containing nothing but scores and scores of filing cabinets. There was a sign that said: RECORDS AND CLASSIFICATION DEPARTMENT – AUTHORIZED ACCESS ONLY.

"Waste of time. Let's keep going down," said Stench, already turning back towards the door and the corridor beyond.

"Just hold on a minute," said Stargazer. She walked over to the nearest filing cabinet and pulled it open. The drawer was full of carefully ordered papers.

"Come on, Stargazer," hissed Stench. "We haven't got much time."

"This might be important," replied Stargazer, urgently searching through the papers. She sat cross-legged on the floor and started flinging pages around to try to make sense of what was there.

"Oh my," she said, after she had examined some of the papers. She stared around her at the mess on the floor.

"What is it?" asked Stench, slowly following her gaze. When she realized what she was looking at, her mouth fell open.

The floor was covered not just in papers but in photographs – photographs of boys, girls, women and men. Thousands of them. Many of them they did not recognize, but some they did. They were photos of girls who had once been at the Institute. Here at last was the key to what happened to the girls when they left the Institute.

Gingerly Stargazer picked up a picture of a girl she remembered, a very jolly hard-working Y girl who always did what she was told and kept out of trouble. Underneath the photograph was her number, and then a lot of other numbers. There were her height, her weight, her age, the colour of her eyes. The details went on for ever, to an almost insane extent. The size of the girl's feet. The colour and texture of her hair. Distinguishing marks and scars. An endless list of meaningless details. There was a sheet accompanying these details, on headed notepaper:

THE INSTITUTE: A DIVISION OF THE TEN CORPORATIONS
AUTHORIZED BY THE CITY BOSS

SUBJECT REPORT

The subject has proved to be a good and conscientious worker at the Controller's Institute and has produced, during her time there, a significant profit contribution. We have now approved her transfer to our partners, the Adult Institute, where she remains. After a difficult period of settling in, as is normal when inmates are transferred to the post-adolescent sector, severe discipline was necessary to ensure her inevitable acquiescence. She is now once again a productive member of the Adult Institute, operating as a bullet-primer in the central weapons factory to help in the ongoing armed struggle against out of Cityers and different-godders.

We confirm she will stay on an indefinite basis and help produce a significant increase in turnover.

Stargazer couldn't read any more. She picked up another report – this time of a boy. It was the same story. And another girl, and another boy. It was *all* the same story.

There was only one place the orphans and the lost ones and the wanderers and refugees and vagabonds and outsiders went when they grew up. And it wasn't back to their families. It was to another institute, just as bleak and hopeless as the one they came from. And no one in the City – no one anywhere in the world – was taking any notice.

Stench wanted to break down there and then. "There's no escape ever," she said despairingly.

"Not unless we do something about it ourselves," said Stargazer in a suddenly steely voice that Stench had never heard from her before. "Pick up as many of these pieces of paper as you can and put them in your pockets."

Stench, being a huge girl, had an enormous coat with about five great pockets, so she was able to cram scores of reports into them. Then, aware that time was running out, they hurried back out into the corridor and down more and more levels of the Pit until they reached what seemed to be the very bottom.

Stargazer let out a hiss. "Shh," she said, and Stench stopped dead.

That Which Must
Not Be Forgotten

Always be brave.
Always be yourself.

Little Fearless

From where she stood in the shadows, Stargazer could see someone sitting outside a cage of metal bars. It was Bellyache. She could not see inside the cage, but she knew that someone was in there, because Bellyache was talking to them.

"I don't know why I have to be stuck down here on the day of the big inspection. It's all your fault. If you hadn't tried to run away, I wouldn't be here. What was the point? Look where you've got yourself."

There was a murmur from the other side of the bars.

"Come and get you! You think they'll come and get you! Listen. They don't even remember you. They don't even know who you are!"

Another murmur, fainter this time.

"Why don't they remember you? Because you don't *exist*. Because you don't *matter*. They don't even believe you existed in the first place. They think you're just a story. I've told you before. I've told you a million times. When will you get it? You're no one. No one. *No one*."

This time only silence answered Bellyache's terrible words.

Stargazer felt anguished and fearful, but excited that they were so close to rescuing Little Fearless.

Bellyache continued droning on. "The other X girls get all the fun. I'm the only one who—"

But Bellyache never finished her sentence, because Stench had clamped her hand over her mouth.

"Sometimes I wish you would look on the bright side of things for a change," said Stench, and with that she whipped Bellyache's leather scourge from her belt, stuffed it in her mouth, and secured it in place with a handkerchief, then produced some string and tied her up.

Bellyache lay on the floor, spluttering and writhing. "Peace and quiet at last," said Stench.

Stargazer was fumbling at Bellyache's belt, where there was a big brass key attached – the key to Little Fearless's cell.

Stargazer unlocked the door and pushed it open. She saw a small figure lying on a plain wooden bench on the other side of the cage. The figure was so thin and pale, it was hard to know if it was Little Fearless or not. Her hair had grown back a little bit but was dirty and tangled, and she wore an old pair of striped pyjamas that looked like they had never been washed. Only when she opened her eyes to reveal one brown eye and one blue eye could Stargazer be sure that it was her best friend.

Little Fearless's eyelids flickered as if she couldn't quite make out what she was seeing. Her gaze seemed far away, and clouded. When she did finally raise her head, she looked first at Stench.

Little Fearless was so tired and weak, she could hardly manage to be surprised. "Hello ... number ... number..." She seemed to struggle for a moment. "Whoever you are. Have you come to mock and curse me?"

"No," said Stench. "Of course not."

"I remember you, though I can't remember your name. It was you who helped me escape from the Institute. You were the ... queen of the hills and valleys of the rubbish tips."

Stench looked away, quite unable to speak, so shocked was she at the sight of Little Fearless in that awful hole.

Stargazer was staring at Little Fearless. She felt both joy at seeing her best friend again and horror to find her so pale and faded away. Little Fearless brought her one brown eye and her one blue eye to rest on Stargazer. For a brief moment, a light appeared in them.

"I know you," she murmured. "I'm sure I do. You're not an X girl. You're ... someone. What are you doing down here?"

"Little Fearless, it's me. It's me, Stargazer. I've come to take you away from this place."

Little Fearless's eyelids flickered, closed, then opened again. "I *do* remember you, I'm sure. You used to be my friend when I was ... when I was a real girl."

"Oh, Little Fearless," said Stargazer, and then fell silent.

After a while, Little Fearless spoke again. "The X girls say no one remembers me."

"*I* remember you," said Stargazer weakly.

"I know it can't be true that I have been forgotten. Because I did it all for them. The escaping. To find their families. Do they tell stories about me? What *do* all the girls say about me now that I am gone?" asked Little Fearless.

"They say … they say … I do not know how to tell you," said Stargazer, barely above a whisper.

"They can say I am bad or a liar or a thief. They can say I am a traitor or a fool. These things are untrue so they do not matter."

"They don't say those things," said Stargazer.

"They can say I pick my nose, that I forget to brush my teeth, that I am sometimes stubborn and hot-headed and don't put my clothes away in a tidy pile at night. You can tell me. I shan't mind."

"No," said Stargazer. "They don't say any of those things."

A look of puzzlement passed across Little Fearless's face. Then suddenly, with what appeared to be her last remaining strength, she raised herself up and looked directly into Stargazer's eyes, the brown and blue of her irises seeming to burn with a strange light.

"They *do* remember me – don't they?"

Stargazer hesitated. It was only for half a second, but Little Fearless was watching her face with all that was left of her strength. In the space of that tiny hesitation, Little Fearless collapsed back onto the bench as she saw the truth that was written in Stargazer's eyes.

At that moment, Stargazer stumbled back, stricken with fear and wonder.

Filling her field of vision were three angels. They had come because they had heard a sound – a sound only angels can hear. It was the sound of a human heart breaking.

"What are you looking at, Stargazer?" said Stench.

"Can't you see? Can't you see?" whispered Stargazer, rapt and terrified.

"There's nothing there," said Stench, bewildered.

Little Fearless gave a gasp, and Stargazer saw the three angels descend and lift Little Fearless's spirit out of her worn and racked body.

One was the angel of compassion, whose face was infinitely agonized and perfectly beautiful at the same time.

The angel of courage had a hundred faces. Little Fearless knew every one of them.

The angel of truth had more faces than anyone could count, and many were wonderful, and still more were too terrible to gaze upon.

The three angels rose, the spirit of Little Fearless flickering between them like pale fire.

Stargazer suddenly began to speak all in a rush, as if she could call Little Fearless back.

"Of *course* they remember you. They talk about you all the

time. You're a hero. You're loved by everyone. You've given them all strength. You've…"

Little Fearless's eyes seemed to flicker, and the light in them grew a little fainter.

Then they closed.

Stargazer took hold of Little Fearless and began to shake her, gently at first, then harder and harder. Almost mad with grief, she drew out from inside her coat the white rose she had picked from the rubbish dumps. "I've brought you a white rose, Little Fearless. I know you love them."

The vision of angels had evaporated. There was only thin, dank air. Stargazer held the white rose out towards Little Fearless, close enough to let her smell the scent. She stood like that for a minute without moving, then gently pushed the rose into a lock of Little Fearless's dirty, tangled hair.

"The angels have taken her," said Stargazer softly. "She has returned to the great nothing."

Stench, stunned with grief, did not speak.

Then Stargazer felt something so strong well up inside her that she thought she would fall over. It felt as if all the pain and anger in the world, and all the determination and all the outrage at all the crimes that had ever been committed were inside her. She cried a cry that seemed to reverberate on the surface, far above them. Then she bent and picked up the dead weight of Little Fearless's body in her thin, pale arms.

"Let me carry her," said Stench sadly. "I'm stronger than you."

"No," said Stargazer so fiercely that Stench took a step back. "I owe her this journey."

So it was that Stargazer carried Little Fearless's slack body all the way up the spiral staircase. Her arms felt like lead and her legs felt as if they were going to collapse at any second, but she kept going.

She carried Little Fearless out of the Discipline Block and towards the exercise yard. The air was cold and the sky was brown as a puddle. The great metal walls, although painted pink and covered with fake ivy, seemed as dull and oppressive as ever.

"What are we going to do?" asked Stench.

"We're going to make the other children remember what must not be forgotten any more. Stench! Watch out ahead."

For just at the entrance to the exercise yard, where the inspection was at that moment taking place, was the Whistler. Immediately Stench disappeared into the shadows.

Whistler was whistling:

Who killed Cock Robin?
I, said the Sparrow,
With my bow and arrow,
I killed Cock Robin.

She spotted Stargazer carrying Little Fearless, and immediately began to move towards them. She stopped whistling.

But now another whistle rose up from somewhere.

Ring-a-ring o' roses,
A pocket full of posies,
A-tishoo! A-tishoo!
We all fall down.

And with the "down" the Whistler felt a strong pair of hands force her to the ground and bind her hands. Then a length of sticky tape was fastened across her mouth. Stench stood over her and muttered, "Try and whistle now."

The Whistler turned red with fury. Stargazer, carrying the body of Little Fearless, just walked on. Stench grabbed the Whistler by the collar of her jacket and pulled her through the dirt after her.

The City Boss was standing on a high podium ten yards in front of the first row of girls, talking into a microphone. The podium was covered in lush red carpet in honour of his visit.

The X girls were dotted here and there among the gathering, watching the Y and Z girls carefully for any signs of misbehaviour. Up on the podium with the City Boss and the Controller were Soapdish, Tattle, Beauty and Lady Luck. Their attention was focused on the City Boss, who was making an elegant and nicely crafted speech. The Controller gazed at him in admiration.

Soapdish saw Stargazer first. Then Tattle, then Beauty. They watched, riveted to the spot, their faces frozen in shock. Then, one by one, the eyes of all the Y and Z girls were drawn to the sight of Stargazer, now staggering under the weight of her burden. Although she was exhausted, still she wouldn't give it up. The vidcams swung away from the City Boss to take in this extraordinary vision.

Eventually, almost every eye in the Institute – and many thousands beyond, watching the vidscreen pictures being broadcast in the City – fixed on the tiny child carrying the filthy, broken body.

Stargazer kept walking towards the podium where the City Boss was still blithely talking, oblivious to what was going on below him. She reached the bottom of the steps that led up to the podium. Slowly Stargazer began to ascend.

Transfixed, not one of the X girls moved to stop her. When, finally, the Controller and the City Boss turned to follow the gaze of all the girls, the Controller let out a loud cry of amazement. Then he immediately started yelling at the X girls, while the City Boss looked on, astonished.

"What are you waiting for? Grab them! Get them out of here."

But seeing Stargazer holding Little Fearless's body, and then the Whistler being dragged behind them by Stench, who looked huge, red-faced and extremely determined, not one of the X girls moved a muscle. The Controller stood stock-still, although his eyes swivelled in panic behind his tinted spectacles.

Then Stargazer, her eyes wet with tears, reached the top of the high podium and, still carrying Little Fearless, walked to the microphone where the City Boss was standing. She looked up at him. So fierce was her gaze, he moved away in alarm. She took his place. Then, with her last reserves of strength, she lifted the tiny, wasted form of Little Fearless above her head, and spoke. The voice that came out was enormous, ten times the size of her normal voice. The small-ness of her frame meant she could not reach the microphone, but everyone within the four walls could still hear her, as clear as a bell.

"Here she is! Here is the girl that doesn't exist!"

She laid Little Fearless gently on the red carpet at her feet, then straightened up again.

"Look at her. She's so cold and dead and *real*. Remember her. Because in forgetting her, you have destroyed her.

"You have lied to yourselves in forgetting her. You have lied in this place that is made out of lies. You have lied because you thought that if you did it long enough, and hard enough, you would escape this place and become real people. But that's a lie too. I've got proof that the only place we're going after we grow up is another house of nowhere."

Stench let go of the Whistler, took from her pockets the reams of papers that she had picked up from the Pit and flung them into the crowd. The girls immediately broke their lines to grab them. As they read the documents, there were mutterings of anger, which grew, then faded. There was a silence that seemed to go on for ever.

The City Boss tried to leave the podium, but found his way blocked by Tattle, Soapdish, Beauty and Stench. Tattle, eyes filled with shame and grief, had been the first to rip the X letter off her lapel. Soapdish, then Beauty, quickly followed suit.

The Controller, momentarily panicked, fell to his knees and began praying to Eidolon. Stargazer looked down at him with sorrow and disdain.

"You should not pray to Eidolon. Or Ormazd, or any other god. You should pray to the stars, to the universe, for ourselves and for our lives, brief and imperfect as they are. Give thanks for the astonishing miracle that there is something rather than nothing. That we exist at all in the endless void. We should worship one another. We should worship our sameness as well as our uniqueness. We should worship what makes us truly human. Compassion. Courage. And truth."

Stargazer's words echoed around the walls of the Institute, met only by silence. It was the Controller who broke it. He was gazing upon the face of Little Fearless. It seemed that only now did he recognize her. He rose unsteadily and he spoke a single word, in a cracked, heartbroken voice.

"Fearless."

At that single sound, the girls blinked. It was as if all at once they had awoken from a dream.

Tattle was the first to echo the Controller's cry. "Little Fearless!"

Then Soapdish and Beauty. "Fearless! Fearless!"

Within seconds, the whole of the Institute were shouting at the top of their voices.

"Fearless! Fearless! Fearless!"

Outside the Institute, thousands of people were demonstrating, and they had been getting restless. A counter-demonstration was taking place that had been organized by the City Boss. These stooges had been shouting that the tears were forgeries, just tap water mixed with salt.

Then a man dressed in the vestments of a priest stood up. He spoke, and his voice soared above the throng.

"I remember this girl," said the priest. "She came to see me too, just as she came to see John. She tried to tell us about the Institute."

Here he nodded at the man John, who had helped to organize the demonstration, and who had arrived in his huge rubbish lorry festooned with banners that read STOP THE TEARS NOW.

"She asked for help. I am ashamed to say I did not help her, because she was dirty and bedraggled; and just a child, so I did not believe her. All the same, I have never been able to forget her. Now I feel sure that she was telling the truth."

Now the argument broke out more furiously than before. Such a cacophony of voices was raised that the police, drafted in to keep order, shifted on their feet uncomfortably. They didn't want a riot on their hands.

Then another voice rang out – this time through a police megaphone.

"I too remember this girl," the voice said. "I have not been able to forget her, however hard I've tried. She came to my police station, but I am ashamed to say that I ignored her. I didn't believe her, because she was an outsider, an out of Cityer and a vagabond. But now I have come to believe that what she told me was true."

The crowd looked and they saw, to their amazement, that it was one of the policemen who was speaking. He took off his helmet, threw it on the ground and stamped on it, and joined the thousands of demonstrators demanding an end to the tears.

Suddenly, what seemed like a trickle of rhythmic noise began to gather itself from inside the walls of the Institute. At first it was a thin whisper, but as it began to build, it became louder and louder until it practically drowned out all of the noise of the demonstrators. No one could at first make out what the noise was; then gradually it became clear from the pitch and tone that it was the massed voices of the girls. They were repeating one word over and over.

"Fearless! Fearless! Fearless!"

The noise grew, and the people at the demonstration began chanting too, while the people from the counter-demonstration tried to shout them down.

"We must go into the Institute," shouted the policeman who had thrown off his helmet.

"Yes," echoed the priest. "We can't hide from ourselves any more."

"We'll tear down the gates," cried the man called John.

In front of them were the two vast gates of the Institute, one the shape of a D, the other the shape of a reversed D. When they were closed, they formed the sign of a zero divided into two parts, one painted black and one painted white. John jumped into the cab of his rubbish lorry, revved the engine, and drove it straight through the zero-shaped gates of the Institute, splintering wood and metal like matchwood. The crowd flooded forward, the police helpless to stop them.

Inside, the chanting of nine hundred and ninety-nine girls was echoing around the Institute.

"Fearless! Fearless!"

The City Boss, still on the podium, had a look of fierce panic on his face. He shouted and gestured at the policeman who was at the head of the crowd. He noticed that for some reason, this policeman wasn't wearing a helmet.

"Thank goodness you've come," said the City Boss to the policeman. "The children are running wild. Round them up and put them back in their dormitories."

The place was in chaos. Girls everywhere were starting to tear down the ugly buildings where they had had to live and work and suffer all these years. Some had seized the matches that the X girls used to light cigarettes and had set alight the hated Control Block. Tongues of fire began to appear from the Controller's headquarters.

To the City Boss's amazement, the policeman at the head of the crowd of demonstrators took no notice of his order and instead bellowed right back at him.

"You told us this was a school, a place of re-education and faith. But it is a prison and a place of misery and hopelessness. You did not tell the truth."

The City Boss held his hands out in a gesture that was at once hopeless and desperate. "The truth has many faces," he said.

There was sorrow in the air, and rage, and the threat of violence. To his right, the City Boss was aware of flames rising higher from the Control Block. And all the time the vidcams watched him, broadcasting his every response to the people of the City. He could see that things were out of control, and struggled to find words that would placate the mob and restore his authority. He looked down at the crowd, his features arranged into a picture of regret and contrition. He smoothed down his jacket and patted his hair into place. He shot a long sorrowful glance at Little Fearless, prostrate on the podium a few feet away from him, and spoke to the crowd in a low, plangent voice that nevertheless echoed to the top of the walls.

"Cityzens. A great wrong has been done here. And it is a great wrong for which I cannot shrug off all responsibility.

You elected me as your leader. And I have failed you."

He left a long pause so the crowd could register the genuineness of his sorrow and the humility of his repentance.

"Today, everything has changed. Everything has changed because of this poor, abandoned little girl. I confess – I have been guilty. Not of evil, but of something just as bad. Guilty of ignorance. Guilty of indifference. Guilty of seeing only what I wanted to see."

The crowd cheered, and many of them started to look smug and self-satisfied that they had defeated what they had now decided was the face of all wrongdoing.

But the City Boss gathered himself and looked down at the crowd defiantly. "But before you hang me from the nearest tree and then walk off in triumph, listen to me.

"If I am dirty, then you are not clean. And all the laundries in the world cannot wash our stains away. You voted for me because you were scared. You voted for me because you valued order more than justice. You voted for me because of the secret hatreds in your own hearts. You voted for me so I could carry your sins for you. So don't suddenly tell me that you are all innocent. You wanted this. This is your doing as much as mine. What do you think politicians do? Do you think they are wicked and out to exploit you? You are wrong. They are here to give you what you *want*. That is how they keep their jobs.

"What you wanted was to feel safe. What you wanted was to feel special. What you wanted was to feel like good people. And I gave you those things. Those illusions. Those lies. And now you crucify me for doing your bidding?"

A silence fell over the crowd.

"You are no better than me. I am leaving the City and shall not come back. Then you can elect someone who is as kind, upstanding and virtuous as *you* all are," intoned the City Boss both magisterially and sarcastically.

"There is one last thing for me to do, before I give up the chains of office and return to ordinary Cityzenship once more."

He turned to the Controller, who was huddled in a corner of the podium, his arms wrapped round himself, his face tight with what could have been either grief or terror. It seemed he feared the crowd would tear him to pieces.

"Controller. You are relieved of your duties. You are no longer an employee of the City. You are finished. Just as I am."

The Controller fell to his knees. The City Boss walked slowly down from the podium and then out through the gates, his head held high, his hair sticking up. No one tried to stop him.

The flames had spread now. A north wind had blown them over to the Work Block. The podium itself was in danger of catching fire. Everyone began to flee towards the shattered remains of the great gates.

Stargazer, exhausted, lay slumped beside Little Fearless's body. Stench picked up Little Fearless gently.

"Come, Stargazer," said Stench softly. "It isn't safe here any more."

"I'm coming," said Stargazer. "But there's something I have to do first."

"Hurry then," said Stench. "The whole Institute is going up in smoke."

Stench made her way down the steps carrying Little Fearless's body. Now only Stargazer remained on the podium – along with a broken, slumped figure that sat, head in hands, a few feet away from her.

Stargazer stared at the Controller in astonishment, and even sorrow. There was ash from the fire in his hair, and coating his skin, making him appear even more like a ghost than before. By now the fire had reached the Living Block and was creeping towards the rubbish tips. The Controller was shaking. Stargazer could not help but pity him. She reached out and touched his arm. He shrank back as if he had been burnt.

"It isn't safe here," said Stargazer softly. "You need to leave."

The Controller didn't respond.

"Your what-must-be is now in your own hands. It is your choice. But I just want to know one thing before I go," said Stargazer.

There was a great crack as the central support of the Control Block broke in the heat, and the roof began to fall in. Ashes and sparks were everywhere now.

"Go, girl, go," said the Controller, suddenly breaking his silence urgently. "You must not stay here." He had taken his hands away from his face now.

"Just answer me this," said Stargazer steadily. "Stench – *Lila* – told me something I didn't understand. She said Little Fearless survived longer than anyone else ever kept in the Pit. She said it was as if you were trying to keep her alive. And you always took a special interest in her – always. Why, Controller? She was just another little girl among hundreds. What made her special to you? Why was she different?"

Now flames sprang from the roofs of all five buildings in the Institute. Stargazer could hear Stench, and Tattle, and Beauty, and Soapdish, all yelling at her to leave the podium, and the Institute, before it was too late.

The Controller, still slumped on the floor of the podium, raised his head slightly. He seemed to be looking directly at her. But he said nothing. Stargazer shook her head. It seemed that she was never going to find out this secret. She rose to her feet and moved slowly towards the steps. Flames were licking at the podium's struts.

She threw one last glance at the Controller before she made her escape. And in that final moment, he raised his right hand to his face and slowly, deliberately, removed his tinted spectacles. Orange flames danced in the lenses.

Stargazer stared. In the flickering light she saw for the first time his eyes, the eyes he had concealed all the years he had been at the Institute.

And one was brown. And the other was blue.

Stargazer just stood there, dumbfounded.

The Controller nodded. "It is true," he muttered. "I tried to protect her. But I had to follow the rules, you see. The rules … the rules…"

Now he was babbling. His face was obscured by a pall of grey smoke. He coughed and spluttered.

"Mary was – is – my sister. She was more than a sister – she was a friend to myself and Little Fearless's mother. She promised to look after her and bring her up as her own. But years later they found her and tortured me by bringing her *here*, saying that unless she followed the rules she would be sent away and I would never see her again. But she wouldn't … she wouldn't follow them … she wouldn't *do* it … she was so brave … and now she's … and now she's…"

His face appeared like a spectre through the smoke. Stargazer did not know whether it was that which was making his eyes water, or whether he was truly crying. Then the fumes and burning ash made it too hard for her to see anything at all.

"How can you love someone when you need to crush them… How can you crush someone … when you cannot help but love them?"

This question was left hanging in the smoke and air. Because Stargazer suddenly felt the strong arms of Stench around her waist, and she was carried quickly down the collapsing stairs.

"The Controller ... the Controller!" shouted Stargazer.

But Stench took no notice. "Too late for that. It is his what-must-be."

And she ran, with Stargazer under her arm, towards the great collapsing zero of the gates. Just as she made it outside, the walls themselves fell, and all was flames, and rubble, and smoke.

Within an hour the Institute was little more than a mound of ash.

And the Controller, Oroborous – Little Fearless's father – was never seen or heard of again.

Epilogue

Atonement

In the warm embrace of the Sunlands, five girls sat on a beach staring at the sea. A middle-aged woman with grey-flecked hair was with them. She was quite tall, with pale freckled skin. There was a dark birthmark the size of a fingernail and shaped like a star just visible below her hairline. Her name was Mary. Each of the six figures held a single white rose.

It was late afternoon, and already the sun was slipping beneath the horizon. The sky was a darkening blue, and waves lapped and bubbled a few yards away from where they sat. A sand crab scuttled past and disappeared into a tiny hole.

"Are you OK, Stargazer?" said Jamila, the girl they had once called Beauty, to the delicate girl with the beautiful yellow hair.

She nodded. "Did I ever tell you that I found out what Little Fearless's real name was?" said Stargazer quietly, who had never found out what her own real name was. She liked being called Stargazer anyway.

"You never told me," said the dark-skinned girl holding her small black rag doll. Her name was Maya.

"Or me," said Abigail, the girl they had once known as Tattle.

All the girls fixed their eyes on Stargazer. "She told me," Stargazer said, nodding towards Mary. Mary caught Stargazer's eye and smiled. Stargazer had lived with her ever since she had left the Institute, and they had come to love one another like mother and daughter. Stargazer smiled back, and continued with her story. She had become a wonderful storyteller, almost as good as Little Fearless herself.

"It's an incredible name. Her mother and her father gave it to her when they were freedom fighters. They thought her name would be her destiny. And they were right."

"What was it, Stargazer?" asked Lila, stroking the petals of her white rose.

Stargazer smiled wryly. "It was Hero," she said softly. "Her real name was Hero."

"She was named after the Hero of the ancient tales," added Mary. She looked around at them all kindly, and put her hand gently on Stargazer's shoulder.

The group fell silent. The last rays of the sun illuminated the sea, staining it the colour of rubies.

"It is time," said Stargazer softly.

Slowly, one by one, they made their way to the edge of the sea. Eddies and rivulets of glittering water lapped at their feet.

"It has been a beautiful day," said Mary.

"And like all days for us, now and for ever, it was a gift from Little Fearless. From a true hero," said Stargazer.

As Stargazer said this, Mary took a deep breath and cast the white rose she was holding into the gently lapping waves. One by one the girls followed suit. By now they were all crying – tears of happiness and gratitude and grief mixed together.

Finally Stargazer took her white rose, kissed it once, twice, three times, then threw it into the sea, where it floated gracefully in formation with the others.

"Goodbye, Little Fearless," she said, almost to herself. "You will never be forgotten."

The waves curled into a crest and carried the white roses, away along a red river of light towards the setting sun. The girls joined hands and walked slowly away, back to their families and their homes, back to a city where, if you listened carefully, the voices of the angels of truth, courage and compassion could be heard once more, like a secret refrain whispered by every human heart.

Acknowledgements

First to my god-daughter Sadie Kitson ("Sadie Strongheart"), who nagged me into starting this story back in 2000. Also to my father, Jack; my stepmother, Lee; and my brother Jeff; and my friends Paul and Judy Stafford, who all encouraged me to keep going when I had almost given up. Likewise to Mark Haddon and Jacqueline Wilson, voices in the wilderness as precious as rain for my often faltering imagination and willpower. To Caroline Walsh at David Higham Associates, who finally found a publisher willing to take a risk. To my brilliant editor at Walker Books, Denise Johnstone-Burt, who had the vision and skill to help me to turn *Fearless* into a real book rather than a patchwork of ideas and images. To Christina Østrem at the Portixol Hotel in Mallorca and to Andrew Milton at the Prince Maurice Hotel in Mauritius, who gave me space and time to work. And finally, as always, to Rachael Newberry for just about everything else good in my life.